MARBLE GRANT

NO ONE HAS MORE FUN BEING DEAD

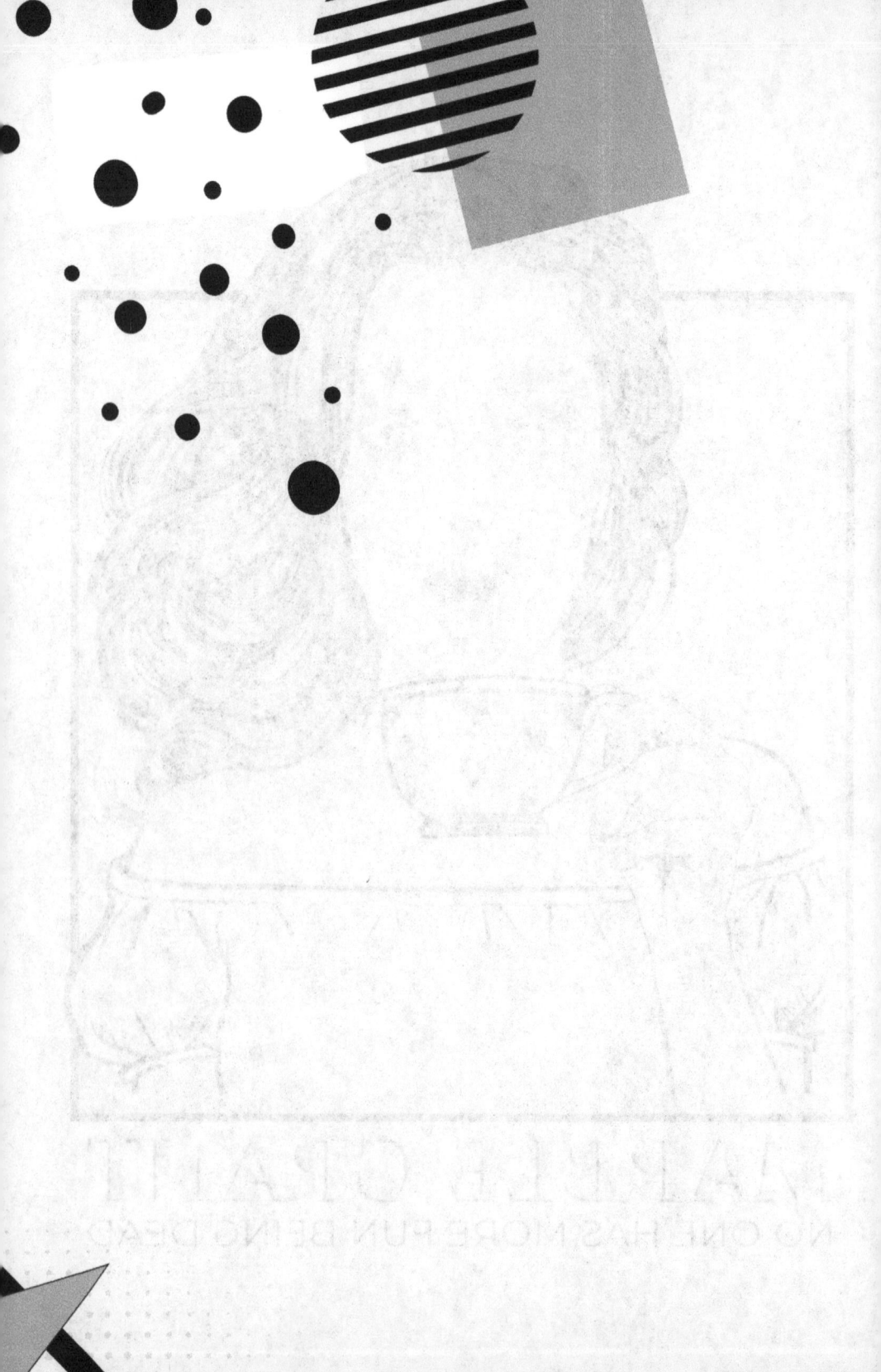

ALSO BY DEAN WESLEY SMITH

THE POKER BOY UNIVERSE

POKER BOY

The Slots of Saturn: A Poker Boy Novel

They're Back: A Poker Boy Short Novel

Luck Be Ladies: A Poker Boy Collection

Playing a Hunch: A Poker Boy Collection

A Poker Boy Christmas: A Poker Boy Collection

GHOST OF A CHANCE

The Poker Chip: A Ghost of a Chance Novel

The Christmas Gift: A Ghost of a Chance Novel

The Free Meal: A Ghost of a Chance Novel

The Cop Car: A Ghost of a Chance Novella

The Deep Sunset: A Ghost of a Chance Novel

MARBLE GRANT

The First Year: A Marble Grant Novel

Time for Cool Madness: Six Crazy Marble Grant Stories

PAKHET JONES
The Big Tom: A Packet Jones Short Novel
Big Eyes: A Packet Jones Short Novel

THUNDER MOUNTAIN

Thunder Mountain

Monumental Summit

Avalanche Creek

The Edwards Mansion

Lake Roosevelt

Warm Springs

Melody Ridge

Grapevine Springs

The Idanha Hotel

The Taft Ranch

Tombstone Canyon

Dry Creek Crossing

Hot Springs Meadow

Green Valley

SEEDERS UNIVERSE

Dust and Kisses: A Seeders Universe Prequel Novel

Against Time

Sector Justice

Morning Song

The High Edge

Star Mist

Star Rain

Star Fall

Starburst

Rescue Two

COLD POKER GANG

Kill Game

Cold Call

Calling Dead

Bad Beat

Dead Hand

Freezeout

Ace High

Burn Card

Heads Up

Ring Game

Bottom Pair

Being Dead (The First Year)

A Marble Grant Novel

Dean Wesley Smith

WMG
PUBLISHING

BEING DEAD (THE FIRST YEAR)
COPYRIGHT © BY DEAN WESLEY SMITH
FIRST PUBLISHED IN SMITH'S MONTHLY ISSUE #50, MARCH 2017
PUBLISHED BY WMG PUBLISHING
COVER AND LAYOUT COPYRIGHT © 2025 BY WMG PUBLISHING
COVER ART COPYRIGHT © LUCKY2084 | DEPOSITPHOTOS

ISBN-13 (EBOOK): 978-1-56146-113-4
ISBN-13 (TRADE PAPERBACK): 978-1-56146-118-9
ISBN-13 (HARDCOVER): 978-1-56146-133-2

TABLE OF CONTENTS

TABLE OF CONTENTS

AUTHOR'S NOTE

Some sections of this book were originally parts or all of Marble Grant short stories that were published in different issues of Smith's Monthly Magazine.

For Kris
Because we need another reason to live in Las Vegas.

BEING DEAD (THE FIRST YEAR)

PART ONE

THE MAKEUP NO LONGER RUNS

CHAPTER ONE

D ying on a first date sucks.

Dying on a blind date sucks even worse.

Especially when your date dies with you. And then goes off through some tunnel of light into the next life or something, leaving you sitting alone, dead, in a dark alley, waiting for your own tunnel of light.

Hands down, the worst ending to any date in recorded history.

The alley we had been forced to go into was blacker than the inside of a latrine, and seeing how it smelled, I would have not been surprised to be in a latrine, but I knew I wasn't since it seemed that being dead meant I could see just fine in the dark.

And smell just fine as well. Holy crap. The nearby Chinese restaurant garbage smelled like my fridge after six

3

days of feeling sorry for myself and laying on the couch and eating take-out without taking out the uneaten food in the original cartons. And no telling how many homeless and drunks had actually used this alley for a bathroom.

I was sitting on a big green dumpster owned by a nearby office, so thankfully it didn't have the odor of the other dumpsters coming up between my legs.

The scum with the greasy black hair and dirty ski parka that had killed us was going through my date's pockets as I sat and watched.

The guy looked skinny and no doubt drug-addicted. His motions were jerky, his eyes darting around him like a rat trying to find a way out of a maze.

My blind date, dear old Handsome Bob, as I had started to think of him for the full thirty minutes I had known him, had caused this mess by thinking he could be a macho asshole or something.

The scum with the greasy black hair had approached us on the sidewalk and Bob had shaken his head and said, "Not now."

We were headed down the street to a nice Italian restaurant that served the best red wine and bread plate this side of New York. And that was going some for the Old Towne section of Boise, Idaho.

Bob was dressed in a clearly expensive silk suit and no tie, while I didn't look so cheap myself. For the date I had put on dark slacks, a white silk blouse with pearls around my neck, and a thin see-through sweater. No bra because I wanted my date to get an occasional peek at what might be offered after dinner if things went right.

Sitting dead in an alley sure wasn't my idea of things going right.

The greasy jerk had pulled out a gun, his hands shaking. Dear old dead Handsome Bob had said, "You don't want to do that."

Bless him.

Clearly the druggie did want to do exactly what he was doing, but I didn't say that. I was busy ramping up one of my super powers.

You see, before I was so suddenly cut down, I had worked as a superhero in the housing and hotel industry. Over the last century I had worked both front desks of hotels and sold real estate. At the moment I was on the real estate side, trying to help out in the booming Boise real estate market.

Amazing the kind of crap that goes on in real estate when big money is involved.

I hit greasy-hair with a full dose of my calming power. The guy was so high on drugs my power actually didn't do anything but make him stop shaking so hard.

He pointed to the dark alley with the gun. "Get in there and then dig out your money."

"And if we say no?" Handsome Bob asked the guy.

Since Bob was almost a foot taller than the greasy-haired druggie, I suppose Bob thought he could bully the situation a little.

Bless dear old now-dead stupid Bob.

I hit the guy with another dose of calming power. I had enough power on a normal day to stop a shouting, irate, pissed-off hotel customer at a front desk and make them smile.

The guy with the gun got calmer, but his pea brain was still set on robbing us. At least I got him to not shoot us right there on the sidewalk because of Handsome Bob's stupidity.

"Let's just give him our stuff and he will let us go," I said to Bob.

"Smart woman," the guy said, smiling and showing a mouthful of rotted teeth.

Actually, I had planned that when we got into the alley I would simply jump us away from this nut and then figure out something to tell dear old Bob.

Bob didn't know I was a one-hundred-year-old superhero and could just teleport anywhere I wanted. Not something you tell someone before a first blind date. Men tended to have sexual problems when they realized the woman they were with was over a hundred.

Bob nodded to me and we walked the twenty steps into the alley, Bob pushing me slightly ahead of him.

Then, as we stopped and turned at just about the point where the rotted Chinese food odor got the worst, Bob went to lunge at the guy.

Handsome Bob went to really, really stupid Bob very quickly.

I was so surprised Bob would do something that idiotic, I didn't react fast enough to jump us out of there.

The guy fired, hitting Bob in the arm.

The bullet went through Bob's flesh and hit me square between the eyes.

Now that was a shocker, let me tell you.

One moment I am standing alive in the alley and the next I am a ghost sitting on a smelly dumpster watching dear old Handsome Bob hold his arm and swear.

The greasy-haired guy was now twitching again. He stared at my body lying there in the alley, clearly getting my wonderful blouse and sweater all stained up with my own blood.

Then he looked at Bob, who was also staring at me, holding his wounded arm and looking sick to his stomach.

Then the guy did what any self-respecting murderer would do. He shot Bob.

Bob slumped to the ground and the guy fired one more shot into Bob's head.

A moment later I watched Bob's ghost stand up, look around, then look up and float off into a white light.

"Nice meeting you jerk-face," I shouted after Bob.

I was pretty sure he didn't hear me.

As I said, the worst ending to a blind date ever.

CHAPTER TWO

The druggie who had killed me and my blind date started through Bob's pockets. The druggie pulled out a money clip and then took Bob's watch. Then he rolled Bob over slightly and took out his wallet.

He pulled out a single-package condom and tossed it aside.

I just shook my head. "Damn, Bob, only one? Where was the confidence? If you had come back to my place, you would have needed at least three just to make it to breakfast."

The greasy murderer clearly didn't hear me. And I had a hunch dead Bob didn't either.

I glanced around. I was still the only ghost in the alley.

Where was my greeting party?

I figured I had become a Ghost Agent, which was why I hadn't gotten the beam-of-light ride. I had never met a Ghost

Agent, but I had heard from my best friend Patty that she and her boyfriend, Poker Boy, had worked with some Ghost Agents just lately to save the world. Seems Patty and her boyfriend were always saving the world, which I must admit I appreciated.

The guy stood and stepped toward my body.

"Hey, not so fast there, jerk-face," I said, jumping down from the dumpster and brushing off my pants.

The greasy-haired slime-ball picked up my clutch purse and went through it. That I didn't much care about. I had a few hundred in there and that was that.

But then he looked around at the mouth of the alley and then looked back at me with that look I had seen scum like him get. Ghost or no ghost, he wasn't touching me, even if I did have a hole in the middle of my forehead.

This night had gone bad enough as it was.

The guy kneeled down beside my body and I took two quick steps at the guy and went to kick him clear across the alley.

Foot went right through him. Charlie Brown would have been proud of my form, though. I didn't end up on my back.

However, when my foot went through the guy, I got to read all of his thoughts.

All of what he was about to do to me.

So I closed my eyes and went inside the scum. Now I knew for a fact I was in a cesspool, swimming in the shit that this guy called thoughts. If I got out of here I would need about ten showers.

If ghosts took showers.

As he reached for my right breast, I shouted at the top of my lungs, "No!"

And trust me, I can be loud.

Just ask anyone who sat beside me at a Broncos' football game.

And I was inside the guy when I shouted.

Slime-bucket grabbed his head and rolled over backward, the intense pain striking everywhere.

As he rolled away, I managed to stand my ground and get out of his body. I shook myself, wishing I could forget the memories of what I had just seen in his mind.

It would take twenty showers before I would feel clean again.

The guy was holding his head and screaming and rolling on the ground. Blood was coming out of his ears.

Both ears.

"Wow, what did you do to him?" a voice behind me asked.

I turned around to see a handsome couple standing to one side looking shocked. Both were about my height of five-ten, both wore jeans, expensive shirts, and tennis shoes.

"The pervert was about to get his jollies on my dead body, so I climbed inside his head and shouted as loud as I could."

Both of them laughed.

Then the woman stepped forward. "I'm Jewel and this is Tommy. We came to help get you used to being a ghost, but guess you are doing just fine."

I shook both their hands, happy as hell I had company.

"I'm Marble Grant. And got a hunch I'm going to need a lot of help."

"Someone close to you?" Tommy asked, pointing at Handsome Bob.

"Knew him for thirty minutes," I said. "Blind date. But I had planned on getting much closer to him after dinner, if you get my drift."

Jewel laughed and Tommy actually blushed a little, which I loved. I had a feeling I was going to like these two.

"I suppose you two are Ghost Agents. Right?"

Both of them looked shocked.

"I was a superhero in the hospitality and real estate side of the world," I said. "Any chance you two know Patty Ledgerwood and Poker Boy?"

"We do," Jewel said.

"You know," I said, "I'm damn hungry and I assume there is a way ghosts eat, so any chance we could get out of this smell and grab a bite and you guys call Patty and have her meet us. I would kind of like to tell her about my sudden death myself, since she has been my best friend for a hundred years now, give or take."

Both of them just nodded.

"Anything we need to do with that guy?" I asked, looking down at the scum who had killed me and Handsome Bob before I had the chance to find out if the handsome part went all the way to Bob's southern regions.

Greasy hair was still rolling on the dirty concrete, holding his ears and screaming. He was losing a lot of blood through his fingers. I clearly had done some damage.

"I think he's finished," Tommy said, laughing.

"Yeah," Jewel said. "Got to remember that trick."

With that we jumped to a place I knew well and loved, the Golden Nugget Buffet in downtown Las Vegas.

Now I knew I was really going to like these two.

Chapter Three

The Golden Nugget Buffet had been decorated in all warm brown cloth and polished brass. Plants ringed the outside of the side part of the dining room nearest the escalator and the tables were solid, as were the chairs.

My hand went right through a chair as I tried to pull it out and Jewel did it for me.

"You'll learn how to actually move some physical matter, but you don't want to do that too often because people start to get spooked."

"I'll bet," I said.

Tommy jumped away to find Patty, and Jewel led me up to the wonderful smelling food. The images from the murderer's head were slowly fading, something I was very grateful for.

"Be careful to not run into anyone," Jewel said, indicating the six people around the large buffet area. "You end up reading their thoughts."

"Yeah, learned that with the guy who shot me," I said.

Jewel showed me how to pick up a plate, which was actually just the ghost component of the plate, and how to take food from the buffet.

In five minutes of filling a ghost plate with ghost food, I managed to not run into anyone alive, which sort of felt like a victory. I called it the dance of the living. A living person came toward me, I stepped sideways and went around them.

Jewel did the same, seemingly without noticing.

Back at the table, I bit into a piece of prime rib and damn near had an orgasm right there at the table.

Jewel just smiled as I moaned and kept on eating the fantastic tasting food.

"I remember the food being good here," I said after a few bites, "but never this good."

"Everything is better when you are a ghost," Jewel said. "Food tastes better, emotions are more powerful, and the travel and living is easier."

"Sex?" I asked.

"As the joke goes," Jewel said, smiling, "it's to die for."

"Oh, no," I said. "I had enough trouble controlling myself when I was alive."

Jewel just laughed and at that moment Tommy appeared.

"Patty is in Poker Boy's office," Tommy said. "Let's just

grab some food and jump there. She's expecting us but doesn't know why yet."

It dawned on me why Patty couldn't jump here. She was still alive. Anyone in the restaurant would see her arrive and then talk to no one. Not a good idea.

Tommy headed for the buffet. I really needed to pee, but instead I kept eating as we waited for him. Damn, the food was so good. I was going to be lucky to not gain a ton of weight now that I had died. I needed to remember to ask Jewel and Tommy how they stayed so thin.

After Tommy came back with a full plate of food, he jumped the three of us and our food and drink to what I assumed was Poker Boy's office, although I had never been there.

In fact, the place was like a legend.

But I had heard it was something special and I had heard right. The office wasn't really an office. It was more like a tile platform floating in the air a thousand feet over the Strip.

All four walls were freaking clear glass with a wood railing about waist high all the way around.

Without that railing, I would have been so afraid of falling off that slick checkered tile floor, I would have been clinging to the furniture and screaming like a ten-year-old girl not wanting to go see her uncle.

And I was dead, so pretty certain the fall wouldn't kill me again.

Still, scary damn place and now I really had to pee.

I made my heart stop racing and looked around.

In the very center of the room was this huge 1950s style diner booth, with a scarred tabletop and red vinyl booth seats on three sides. The thing was big enough to hold ten people if the people really liked each other.

There were half-a-dozen chairs around the room that could be pulled up to the open end of the booth I suppose, but three of them just sat facing out over the incredible view of the city.

And wow, what a view. I had always loved the lights of Las Vegas. Just never seen them from the air like this before.

"Marble," Patty said as we appeared. "Tommy said you needed to talk with me. Everything all right? You could have just called you know?"

"Not sure I knew how exactly," I said, smiling at my best friend.

Jewel laughed as she set her food and mine on the booth table.

Patty was wearing her MGM Grand Front Desk uniform of dark slacks, tan blouse and a lighter tan vest. She had her long hair pulled back and was as stunning as ever.

Patty frowned, something I had rarely seen her do in a century.

I glanced at my food on the booth table, then turned back to my friend. "Got myself killed while on a blind date about thirty minutes ago."

Patty's eyes went totally round. "Are you all right?"

"Pretty sure I'm dead," I said, laughing. I pointed to my forehead. "Bullet right there did the trick."

Patty looked like she was about to cry.

"Can I hug her?" I asked, glancing back at Jewel.

"She's a superhero," Jewel said, "and she can see you, so sure, don't know why not?"

I stepped toward Patty and she hugged me so hard, I wasn't sure I would be able to breathe.

And I hugged her back.

I guess, for the first time, it was sinking in that I had really died.

I was still here but I was dead.

That just sucked.

Except for the part about the food tasting so much better.

CHAPTER FOUR

After we got done with all the wonderful hugging, we all sat down in the big booth and I went back to eating and telling Patty about what happened with me and my idiot blind date, Handsome Bob.

"So what's next for me?" I asked after I was done eating and telling Patty everything. "Clearly the powers that be didn't want me to go with my blind date into the big beyond."

Jewel shook her head. "Honestly don't know. To my knowledge, there has never been a superhero become a Ghost Agent before."

"Training on your new ghost powers will be first priority, most likely," Tommy said.

"And seeing which of your superhero powers you still have," Jewel said.

I nodded and sort of sat back and looked at Patty. "Anyone around who might know why I am still sitting here in this diner in the sky?"

"I suppose I would know," Laverne said, appearing at the end of the booth.

She was smiling.

Thank the heavens she was smiling.

Now I had been a superhero for a hundred years, yet I had never met Laverne, the woman who ran it all.

Somehow, when I realized who she was, I managed to not pee my pants. Total victory at that moment.

Standing right beside me was the most powerful god in all of the world, Lady Luck herself, about to tell me why I had been spared from the tunnel to the next place.

"Thanks," Patty said as Laverne pulled over a chair to sit at the end of the table.

"Great timing as always," another woman said from behind me as she came around carrying some fantastic-smelling baskets of fries and massive milkshakes that could put a dragon into a diabetic coma.

"I'm Madge," the woman said to me.

"Nice meeting you," I managed to say as the woman in a far-too-tight blue uniform turned and headed for a door behind the booth.

"You too," the woman said over her shoulder and vanished through the door.

Laverne was already working on the fries in front of her. All I could do was stare at the shake in front of me.

There was absolutely no doubt I was going to gain a billion pounds being dead if I wasn't careful.

"So," Patty said as she grabbed a fry as well. "I assume it was just Marble's time. Right?"

Laverne nodded. "We all have our time to head on to whatever is on the other side. But the Powers That Be thought you, Marble, would make a good addition to the Ghost Agent ranks. So they held you back."

"Thanks," I said.

I couldn't believe I had actually said something to Lady Luck.

I bit into a hot fry and again just about had an orgasm right there in front of Lady Luck. Damn that would have been embarrassing. And more than likely messy since I really needed to pee and hadn't figured out where a restroom might be floating a thousand feet in the air.

"I had nothing to do with it," Laverne said. "But I tend to agree, I think a former superhero in the Ghost Agent ranks would be fantastic. We have a superhero teamed up with a Ghost Agent up in Oregon and that has been working wonderfully."

"I'm looking forward to seeing what I can do to help," I said. I wanted to take another fry, but didn't think I should risk it at the moment.

"Actually," Laverne said, glancing at Jewel and Tommy, "Marble, you won't be the only superhero headed to Ghost Agent status. You are going to get a partner."

"Oh, no," Patty said. "Who is dying?"

Laverne kept eating as if such a question was an everyday happening. I sort of sat stunned.

"Can't say," Laverne said. "Against just about every rule in the book."

Patty nodded and sat back, looking worried.

"But we will know just about when it happens," Jewel said. "We'll be there to help with the transition."

Laverne nodded and glanced at Patty. "And don't worry, it isn't any of Poker Boy's team."

Patty let out the air she had clearly been holding. "Thank you."

Laverne just smiled.

I was starting to think I might really like Lady Luck if I ever got the chance to know her better. I can say this floating office was starting to grow on me. I just wished it had a bathroom.

"We have some big challenges coming up," Lady Luck said. "A couple ex-superhero Ghost Agents just might be exactly the team we need to help out."

"So I need to get training until my partner arrives," I said.

Laverne nodded. "Exactly."

Laverne took one more fry and stood. "Welcome to the Ghost Agents side of things."

"Thank you," I said, nodding.

With that, Lady Luck vanished.

The four of us sat there for a moment in silence.

"At least I didn't lose you tonight," Patty said.

"Yeah, pretty happy about that myself," I said, smiling.

My best friend for the past hundred years smiled back.

"Tonight is a start," Jewel said. "A good start."

I laughed. "You know, when I became a superhero, I never had an origin story. I always thought every superhero should have an origin story. But for me it just sort of happened over a long period of time."

Patty smiled. "Yeah, same for me."

"But now that I am a superhero Ghost Agent, I guess tonight you would call my origin story."

The three of them laughed.

"From wanting sex with Handsome Bob to getting shot to meeting Lady Luck, an origin story to remember."

"That it is," Patty said, laughing. "That it is."

Then I smiled at my best friend. "I just don't want to add peeing in your boyfriend's office to the story. A restroom close by?"

Jewel laughed and said to Tommy. "We'll be right back. I've got an agent to train on how to use a restroom without actually touching anything."

"Don't eat my fries," I said to Patty, who just laughed.

And with that my Ghost Agent training started.

Potty training. Who knew?

CHAPTER FIVE

Who knew that so much training went along with being dead. I felt like a kid again, only I didn't have to start all the way back in diapers.

But I did have to learn how to use restrooms, since it seemed ghosts had to pee and eat and everything else and for a woman having the lid up on a toilet was a critical factor. I couldn't lift a lid yet.

One of the very first lessons I learned was to check to see if some woman was in a stall before sticking my head through the stall door to see if the lid was up.

Learned that lesson the hard way. Ugly hard way. I'll never get that sight or that smell out of my memory. Four hundred pounds, almost nude, and clearly the poor woman had eaten something very, very wrong.

Rotten fish and dead animal under a bridge kind of wrong.

Luckily the poor woman didn't hear me gasp, cough disgustingly, and stumble back and through the wall and right into the men's room. Let me tell you, that morning I heard noises from the stalls in that men's room I didn't know were possible for a human to make.

A girl could get real traumatized being dead, of that there was no doubt. Jewel said when I returned to the breakfast table that I was almost ghost white. Ghost-white skin didn't match my purple hair or my bright yellow blouse no matter how dead I was.

I also had to figure out how to eat and start learning how to actually touch something physical and move it. You know, things like toilet lids. My trainers of the dead, Jewel and Tommy, said that would take me time.

As with everything else they taught me, they had been right.

After three months of training, I knew how to control live people, knew how to eat and dress with ghost food and clothing, and could get around pretty well by teleporting, just as I had as a superhero.

I was feeling pretty darned good about it all, actually.

I also had learned more about sex by being inside of people's heads than I had learned dating men and women both for over a hundred years. Wow, some folks out there really were kinky. I mean I liked to experiment and I sure enjoyed sex, but some of the stuff I saw in people's minds just made me look away.

Damn tough when you are in a person's mind, let me tell you.

My best friend of the last hundred years, Patty, who was still alive and a superhero like I used to be before a bullet implanted itself into my forehead, helped me get a nifty and large two-bedroom condo in Las Vegas on the fifth floor of the Ogden Building downtown.

Her boyfriend, Poker Boy, seemed to have more money than Fort Knox and he bought the place and all the furniture and fixtures I wanted, as well as all my clothes.

I kissed him on the cheek and told him I doubted I would ever be able to pay him back. He had just laughed.

Patty told me later that was his embarrassed laugh. Then she told me he would never miss the money in the slightest. Seems Fort Knox couldn't match his money. Playing poker and investing the money smartly over time had clearly been good for him. Besides, he figured the condo was an investment since I sure couldn't own it or sell it.

Patty had helped me shop for clothes. Ghosts could take and wear the ghost part of any clothing. But if I actually had the physical clothes hanging in my closet, I could always wear the ghost part of the outfit any time I wanted.

And no damn laundry. I just tossed the dirty clothes in a basket and a day or so later the ghost clothes vanished. They went back and joined their real part in the closet, all neat and fresh just as I had bought it, for me to use again.

Didn't get better than that.

So Poker Boy had given me and Patty an unlimited credit card and I now had my bedroom and a hall closet full of brand new clothes and shoes and sexy underwear, even though I doubted the sexy part of the underwear was going to get used any time soon.

The ghost part of the vibrator that Patty helped me buy got used regularly to cure that old tingling, especially when I happened to stumble into an attractive man or woman and read their thoughts and their likes and dislikes in the bedroom.

Those images from those people's minds made for some good before-sleep fantasy workouts with that vibrator.

Yeah, kind of being a voyeur, I know, but a ghost does what a ghost can do.

I decided to not fill my extra bedroom closet with clothes just yet. Never knew when someone alive or dead would need a guest room. So Patty and I furnished it with a large bed, wooden dresser, and a reading chair with lamp.

One thing for certain, it was great to have rich live friends when a person was a ghost. Made living a ton more comfortable. I had had a nice place in Boise before I died, but nothing like this condo.

Everything in it was ultra modern and clean and the couch and chairs in the living room were actually comfortable. I had dozed off numbers of times already watching movies on that couch.

The kitchen was enough to make me want to learn how to

cook, even though I lived in a city with some of the best restaurants in the world where I could get food from at any moment.

I had gotten into a habit at night for dinner of going to a new restaurant and bringing back to my place one of their specialties. Something different every night sure kept things interesting in the food department.

The view of the condo was toward the Strip and the balcony had a glass table and five surprisingly comfortable chairs. On warm evenings I usually ate dinner out there, just enjoying the feel of being lucky.

Yeah, I know, I had been killed and I was now a ghost.

Still I felt damn lucky.

CHAPTER SIX

I was enjoying one of the sweetest-tasting peach daiquiris on my balcony just before sunset four months after I had died when Jewel and Tommy appeared.

I had yet to jump to get dinner, but I had plans on trying a barbeque plate from a place in the MGM Grand where Patty worked. She said it was wonderful.

Jewel and Tommy both had on their normal jeans, expensive shirt and blouse, and tennis shoes. Together they were the most attractive couple I had ever met. Stunning model-like looks. Tommy had those wide shoulders of a cop and Jewel was thin and trim and always looked perfectly together.

Did I mention they were also two of the smartest people I had ever met as well? Both had higher degrees and Jewel had been a medical doctor. And on top of all that, they were just flat nice people. Go figure.

"Sorry to bother you without checking ahead," Jewel said. "But we figured you would want to join us."

I took a long drink off the daiquiri as I stood. "You know me. Always up for an adventure. Where are we headed?"

"Your partner is about to join us," Jewel said.

"Damn right I want to be there," I said, laughing.

I had been hearing since almost the moment I discovered I was a ghost that I would have a ghost partner at some point joining me. I knew nothing at all about this person. No one would say a word since the person was still alive. So it had sort of been one of those nagging events coming that I had mostly just put out of my mind.

Jewel smiled. "Then let's go."

And the next thing I knew I was standing in a hot, dry desert on the shoulder of a two-lane paved road. The sun looked exactly like it had from my condo balcony, so I figured I was somewhere in the desert southwest.

"We're fifty miles to the north of Las Vegas," Tommy said.

The two-lane highway stretched off into the distance in both directions. There was not a building or a soul in sight. A slight breeze was doing some wonderful things with my nipples through my thin blouse and my long purple hair was blowing slightly around my shoulders.

I had on my evening kick-around-the-condo sweat pants and tennis shoes. I certainly hadn't dressed for this occasion.

We stood there on the edge of the road in the fading light for a good minute with nothing happening.

"We in the wrong place?" I finally asked.

Never was one for just standing and waiting. Another nice thing about being dead, I seldom had to stand and wait for anything.

Tommy pointed to the north. In the distance I could see a single light coming toward us. That would be the first car to pass us since we got here.

Only it became clear fairly quickly that it wasn't a car, but a motorcycle. And it was moving at an insane speed.

As the motorcycle was about to flash past us, a coyote jumped up from the ditch beside the road and the motorcycle hit the creature square in the side. Neither the poor coyote, nor the motorcyclist, had even an instant to react.

I watched as the motorcyclist in black leathers and black wrap-around helmet went sailing past us about thirty feet in the air over our heads.

The impact of the cyclist hitting the road was an awful sound.

The cyclist started doing uncontrolled cartwheels along the pavement.

To one side of us the remains of the coyote landed in two parts.

On the other side of the road the big black motorcycle was doing cartwheels out into the desert brush, flipping parts in all directions like a stripper shedding clothes.

I wanted to be sick.

That accident had to be one of the most horrid things I had ever witnessed.

Hands down the most violent.

Being a superhero in the real estate and hospitality areas didn't much call for extreme violence.

CHAPTER SEVEN

The three of us stood there on the side of the road without talking. I don't think any of us had expected the intense violence of that accident. That cyclist must have been going well over a hundred miles per hour.

The body finally slid to a stop about a football field's distance away from us and a moment later the cyclist in all black, still wearing a helmet, was sitting on a rock to the right of the road, closer to us than the body.

"That's our signal," Jewel said and led the way as the three of us walked up the road toward the cyclist.

I was working on taking deep breaths, pushing the image of that accident out of my mind so that I could focus forward. This person was supposed to be my future partner. Certainly he or she was someone who liked to take risks.

If nothing else, that might get interesting at times.

The three of us stopped near the cyclist who looked up, face hidden by the black faceplate on the helmet. Then two gloved hands came up and took off the helmet, shaking loose long blonde hair.

Sitting there on the rock, newly dead, was one of the most attractive women I had ever seen. She had deep blue eyes, high cheekbones, and a short nose.

She looked completely stunned and even with that look she was beautiful.

"What happened?" she asked, looking at us.

"You had an accident," Jewel said.

The woman shook her head and took off her gloves, tucking them into her helmet in a practiced move.

"Not likely. At that speed I would be dead. And I don't even have a scratch on me."

None of us said a word. We just let her slowly figure it out for herself.

Finally Jewel introduced the three of us.

"I'm Sally Glass," the woman said.

"Where are you from?" Jewel asked.

I was impressed at how calm and level Jewel sounded. I was still having trouble getting my heart under control from the violence of that crash and also the beauty of the woman sitting on the rock in front of me.

I was attracted to women as much as I was to men. And clearly Sally was my type.

Also, her name sounded very, very familiar.

The more I looked at Sally under those motorcycle leathers, the more I realized she was about my size and shape at five-eight. That would be helpful in getting her some clothing.

The nagging feeling that I knew her kept getting stronger like a bad itch in a place I couldn't scratch.

"Boise," Sally said, pointing back north. "Wanted to spend a few days in Vegas and clear my head a little."

"I was from Boise," I said, working to keep my voice as calm as I could. "I worked real estate there among other things."

Sally nodded. "Banks and construction, among other things. And you look very familiar."

"I was thinking the same for you," I said.

Jewel glanced at me and nodded. She was about to say something when Patty appeared.

I suddenly felt very relieved that a real live person was here.

"Patty," Sally said, standing and sounding happy.

"Hi, Sims," Patty said.

The two women stepped toward each other and hugged on the edge of the road.

"I was hoping to get to see you on this trip," Sims said.

The moment Patty said "Sims" I knew who this woman was. She was also a superhero in the banking side. Patty had always talked about getting the three of us together at some point, but it had never happened. Seems Sims and Patty had met about fifty years ago when Sims became a superhero.

But now we had finally met, in the middle of the desert, with Sims' broken body crumpled in a pile beside the road about fifty steps away.

"So what is this all about?" Sims asked.

"You had an accident," Patty said.

"That's what they—Oh, crap, I'm a Ghost Agent."

Sims suddenly looked like she needed to sit down again and Patty moved to Sims' right and I went to her left side and we braced her.

"You are a Ghost Agent now," Jewel said. "Tommy, Marble, and I are all three Ghost Agents. Marble is also a superhero like you."

"I'm dead?" Sims asked. "Really dead?"

Jewel nodded and pointed to the body.

Sims looked around until she spotted her own body and then nodded. "I knew there was no way I could survive an accident at that speed. Did you see it? Must have been spectacular."

"Violent," I said, enjoying holding her up a little more than I probably should have at that moment. "And I'm afraid to say the coyote you hit didn't make it either."

Sims laughed and shook her head.

"So you hungry?" Jewel asked.

Sims frowned. "I was really hungry before all this. One of the reasons I was going so fast. And I still am. Do ghosts eat?"

"Take it from a newly-made Ghost Agent as well," I said. "We do eat and everything tastes better than you can imagine."

Jewel and Tommy both nodded to that.

Sims looked at me, then nodded. "You were killed in a double murder in an alley in Boise about four months ago. Right?"

I nodded.

"I remember when that happened and was surprised Patty wasn't more upset than she was when I heard it was you."

I laughed. "She's been helping me. Wait until you see the condo she and Poker Boy got me to live in."

"Can't wait," Sims said and smiled at me.

I damn near melted right there in the desert. Working with this woman was going to be heaven. And if she didn't like women as a sexual partner, my poor ghost vibrator would get a regular workout.

Patty looked at me. "All right if Sims borrows something to wear?"

I laughed. "Never a problem. I think we bought me more than enough."

Patty turned to Jewel and Tommy. "How about the three of us meet you at the Golden Nugget buffet in fifteen minutes?"

"We'll be there," Jewel and Tommy said and vanished.

A moment later we were out of the slight wind of the desert and in my condo.

The idea of getting to help train Sims to be a Ghost Agent over the next months had me excited to say the least. But watching her strip naked in my bedroom topped any thought of that being the most exciting.

Her body was amazingly like mine. Thin hips and small breasts. Only she was a natural blonde where I was a complete brunette when I didn't color my hair one color or another.

And we were almost exactly the same height.

I showed her how to turn on the water in the bathroom so she could take a quick shower. When she came out with wet hair and a towel around her, she looked even more stunning.

"Kind of strange how the towel still just stays on the rack in there while I dry off with this same towel."

"Everything has a ghost component," I said. "Jewel and Tommy will explain everything."

Sims nodded.

"Wait until you taste the ghost component of food," I said. "Better than anything you have ever tasted."

"I am so starved right now cardboard might taste good," she said and dropped the towel to start to get dressed.

I had to turn away or simply melt into a puddle, she was that beautiful.

And I was that horny.

The only slight imperfection she had was a scar on one hip that someday I would ask her about, but not tonight.

Later that night, as Sims changed clothes once again to get ready for bed in my guestroom, I decided seeing her naked was by far the most exciting thing of the day.

By a long ways.

Two hours later, when she knocked on my bedroom door and came in and asked me to hold her, I knew from here the days would just get better.

44

I had considered myself lucky as it was.

But I remembered that first night after I had died being scared and uncertain about everything. I wish Sims had been there to hold me.

But now I could hold her.

And that was all that mattered.

I had just gotten factors luckier to have her as a partner.

We fell asleep in each other's arms.

And she never used the guest bedroom again.

Dead or alive, that would have been just fine with me.

But honestly, being dead made it even better.

PART TWO

THE FIRST BIG CASE

CHAPTER EIGHT

I loved what I called mornings. Actually, my morning was what most people call noon, but I'm far from most people.

Besides, being dead brought all sorts of privileges.

Right around noon I usually managed to stumble naked to the kitchen, get a cup of coffee from the pot my wonderful Sims, roommate and partner, had started before she left.

Every day I would take a sip, sigh heavily, then stagger with the cup back to the bathroom trying my best to not spill anything, even though it would never make a mess for long on the tile since it was ghost coffee.

By the time I got done in the bathroom and with that first cup of coffee, I was almost human.

Almost.

At least I could be talked to safely at that point.

Since being dead, I had taken to wearing mostly comfortable clothes. Expensive silk blouses, sports bra, jeans that fit my frame, as Sims said, like a stretch glove, and running shoes.

Sims and I put on our "get screwed" dresses once a week and went out on the town to dance and drink. But the rest of the time I could see no reason not to be comfortable.

I got back to the modern, spotless kitchen with white quartz counter, took a wonderful-tasting fresh bagel that Sims had picked up earlier this morning, spread some cream cheese on it, and went to the patio to sit at the glass table there with a second cup of coffee. I would usually just sit there for about a half hour and stare out over Las Vegas.

After that I was really human and completely safe to talk to.

Honest. No matter what anyone said.

Those mornings on the balcony were so special, I couldn't imagine not doing them. Our two-bedroom condo in the Ogden building in downtown Las Vegas had a view to die for, if I wasn't already dead. I could see all the way out the Strip toward the airport as well as the mountains beyond.

At night the lights of the Strip were just dazzling.

This morning the air had a crisp bite to it, which sort of surprised me considering the day was supposed to be a hot one. But the coffee kept me warm enough.

Sims would still be training with Jewel and Tommy this morning. All three of them were morning people. I was a night person, which Sims and I decided would work out great.

She would get up, have time in the condo without me, get out and do some work. We could work together in the afternoon and then we could share the evening together and after she went to bed I would head out to do what we Ghost Agents did.

Our jobs, it seemed, were to help people. Since we could be inside of people's minds and thoughts and control their actions while in there, we knew who was in trouble and who wasn't.

Most of the time we could even figure out fixes or at least help the person some.

And to me, honestly, that felt damn great. I had been a superhero working in real estate and hotels for the last hundred years before I got that bullet in the forehead. Now, as a Ghost Agent, I was managing in a month to do more good than I did in a year as a superhero.

Every day I felt lucky. I know. Sort of bug-crazy. Most people say they are lucky to be alive.

I'm damn lucky to be dead.

Go figure.

And I am even luckier to have met Sims. We just fit together completely and, as she said after two months together, she couldn't imagine how she lived without us together.

I felt the same way exactly.

Plus she was a tiger in bed and every morning she made me coffee and brought me fresh bagels. What more could a dead girl ask for?

Really.

CHAPTER NINE

I was just finishing up my coffee and rinsing out my cup in the sink when Sims appeared beside me.

She kissed me on the cheek.

"Marble, you know you don't have to do that?" she asked, pointing to the cup I had just rinsed and put in the dishwasher.

A ghost element of a glass or dish just vanished in a few hours if we were not touching it. The real cup I had used was still sitting on the shelf.

So there was no need to wash anything. And we had never once started the dishwasher.

I noticed her morning dishes were still in the dishwasher as well as I put my coffee cup in there.

"I know," I said, smiling and pointing at her dishes. "Old habits die harder than we did."

She laughed, then she got that serious look on her face I had come to love.

Sims seemed to have almost no eyebrows. Her long blonde hair was thin and fine and felt wonderful to run my fingers through. And her large blue eyes could pin me to a wall with just a look and take my breath away.

I was starting to realize she might be one of the smartest people I had ever met as well. And devious at times, which matched right into my attitude perfectly. It was a hell of a lot more fun to be devious when the situation warranted.

"Got us a wife beater this morning," she said. "It was his fetish, to beat on women."

I shook my head. "What did you do to the bastard?"

She laughed and grinned. "He thinks of hitting his wife or any woman again, he will automatically punch himself in the nuts."

"Oh, my," I managed to say after I caught my breath from laughing. "Was that fun to watch?"

Sims just smiled and nodded. "He was having breakfast at a café off the Strip, suddenly stood up and punched himself in the nuts. He was still screaming in pain, but starting to recover, when the paramedics got there. One of them was a pretty young woman and our pervert punched himself in the nuts again before they could restrain him."

It took me a full minute to stop laughing. "Damn, wish I could have seen that. We do that a few more times and they might start thinking it is a disease."

"Ball-punchers syndrome," she said.

"A rare but painful disease you can't get shots for."

She laughed at that, then got serious again.

"There's more."

I nodded.

"He was part of a pretty active dark web group that believed all women should be subjects and beaten regularly."

Sims' voice was soft and angry.

I had already learned in our few months together that making Sims angry was never a good plan. She was sweet and gentle almost all the time, but had a core anger that could level a building. Luckily, that anger had not been aimed at me so far. I hoped to avoid that at all costs.

Now I moved over and held her.

I knew that about ninety years ago she had ended up marrying an abuser, so finding an entire network of them that talked about it must have dug up those old memories in a horrific manner.

After a moment I asked, "You had lunch yet?"

She shook her head.

"How about we jump to the Golden Nugget Buffet and figure out a plan on how we're going to take down that group?"

Sims nodded. "Think we can do it? We're just new Ghost Agents and those creeps are spread all over the world."

"We might need some computer help," I said. "There is always a way."

"I hope you are right," she said.

"We'll figure it out," I said, "and then a plague of the puzzling crotch-punching disease will spread over the world."

She laughed and hugged me.

"Just think," I said, pretending to look serious. "The companies that make ice bags to take down swelling are going to make a fortune."

We were both still laughing when we arrived at the buffet to plan.

CHAPTER TEN

Turns out Sims' worry about taking down this group being difficult was justified.

We started off in the hospital with the original crotch-puncher Sims had run across this morning. His hands were both strapped to the bed and his normally pasty face was red.

He looked like he was drugged a little and was just staring at the tile ceiling.

What looked like ice bags were strapped over his crotch. If we could pull this off, my joke about the ice bag makers might actually be right. Who knew?

Crotch-puncher's wife, a woman who looked like she had been beautiful once, sat beside his bed silently. Now she had her mousy brown hair pulled back off her face and wore clothing that clearly hid her arms and neck. She seemed almost shrunken in on herself.

"We got to do something to help her," I said as we arrived.

Sims nodded. Then she said, pointing at crotch-puncher, "You ready? It's not pretty in there."

I could tell the woman I was completely in love with was having issues.

"As much as I will ever be," I said. "And you know you don't need to go back in that creep's head again. I can get what we are looking for just fine. Why don't you help the wife?"

Sims nodded, looking relieved. "Thanks."

"That's what partners are for," I said.

Then I turned and went inside crotch-puncher's body.

Sims had been right. This guy was a bastard at all levels. Hated at work, hated in his neighborhood, hated by his wife. And all caused by his anger. I could see his computer setup in a book-lined study in his home in Los Angeles.

His wife, from his memories, had clearly been beautiful when they met. But he had started hitting her about five years into the relationship and then basically made her a prisoner to his money and anger.

I dug back and got exactly how he logged into the dark web, the group he went to, and so on.

A group of women-haters like I never knew existed. I knew some men hated women, feared women, thought of women as property even in this modern age. I just had never imagined a group that bragged to each other about the violence they had done to their wives.

And not just a few, but from what I could tell the group consisted of hundreds and hundreds just as screwed up as this guy.

We were going to need massive computer help, of that I had no doubt.

I got all the information I could get, then planted a clear command that he would allow his wife to leave him and not contest any divorce.

I saw where Sims had planted the punch-in-the-balls command at the thought of hitting a woman and made it stronger and deeper, a trick that Jewel had shown me how to do.

This guy would never get that command out of his system, no matter how much counseling he took or medical help he got. He would suffer the rest of his life, just as his wife would suffer from what he did to her the rest of her life.

I climbed out of the guy's mind and then did a trick Jewel had taught me to remember the information I needed to remember and let the rest of the memories of that sick mind fade.

A moment later Sims appeared beside the wife.

"I tried to help her," Sims said. "But she is pretty broken. She is going to go find help at a women's shelter here in Vegas and divorce the bastard."

"I made sure he wouldn't fight the divorce and give her the settlement she asks for," I said, hugging my partner.

At that moment the wife stood, life back in her eyes again. She looked at her husband strapped to the hospital bed.

"No one will ever hit me again," she said to crotch-puncher.

With that, she turned and walked out.

I was cheering and Sims was crying.

Crotch-puncher was trying to get his hands free so he could hit himself again.

CHAPTER ELEVEN

Turns out that two Ghost Agents that lived and worked together in Portland, Oregon, were experts in computers.

And hot? Wow, were they hot. The Sunset Kid and Gail, his partner, were the most striking couple I had ever had the chance to meet.

The first time we met them, Sims took my hand and squeezed it.

Then she sighed and I barely could keep from laughing.

Both Gail and Sunset looked like they could have stepped out of a fashion magazine. They dressed much nicer than Sims and I did, with Sunset actually in a silk suit without a tie and Gail in designer clothes.

And they were clearly very much in love.

Later that night at home in Las Vegas, Sims and I talked

about how much fun it would be to join the two of them for a romp in a very large bed. And that got us both hot thinking about it, even though we both knew that would never happen.

Still, a fun night of thinking about it. Put it this way, we messed up our own bed pretty well that night.

Both Gail and Sunset wanted to help the moment they heard what we were trying to do. And said they would also help in setting the crotch-punching command as well once we figured out how to get to the bastards.

Jewel and Tommy were also going to help.

So we had six Ghost Agents on this. All we had to do was figure out how to track all these sick men through their computers.

I was hopeful, Sims doubtful.

Gail and Sunset said it would take them some time to figure it out. They actually went to the crotch-puncher's house in LA and used his own computer and log-in information to get into the group.

Sims and I stayed to our routine, with Sims training with Jewel and Tommy in the mornings while I was still asleep and then I would go out with her and we would see who we could help around Vegas.

There was never a shortage.

At night after Sims toddled off to bed, I went out on my own to see who I could help as well.

Four days after we had talked with Gail and Sunset, they appeared on our balcony with Jewel and Tommy.

Sims and I had been sitting together, planning our day.

Sims got them all some coffee and I got them bagels and the six of us sat on the balcony on a warm Las Vegas afternoon planning.

Gail and Sunset had figured out how to get through the group and they had all the names and addresses of the over seven hundred signed-in users to the sick place.

I suppose it shouldn't have surprised me there were that many members, but it did. For some reason I thought the simple fact of getting onto the dark web would stop most, and then not wanting to brag about being a monster would stop others.

Then I realized that chances are I was right. We were only going to hit the tip of an iceberg.

And that just made me angry.

We all decided we couldn't wait one minute longer because women were in danger out there. It would take us late into the night, but we could get it done.

So we divided the list into three parts and decided we would go in as teams. One person would set the crotch-punching command so deep it would last the rest of the bastard's life.

The other partner would stay out and be there for support. Then at the next bastard they would switch.

We all decided we would also help the wife clean out some of the damage and get to help. And we would make sure that the husband would allow them to leave and not fight the divorce.

It was the least we could do for those poor women.

I liked that plan, but hoped to change it a little once Sims and I got going. I didn't have a history of abuse in my past. The only man who had hit me, I had killed.

Pretty simple solution. He never hit me again, or any woman for that matter.

And no one ever found his body either.

It was 1921, a damn easy time to hide a body.

But Sims had gotten stuck for a time in an abusive relationship early on and it still haunted her. So I planned on doing the most climbing in bastard's heads.

But I knew she would want to do some, just to help clear out some of her past.

And I would be there to support her when she came out of each one of those monsters.

I had no doubt that today might end up being one of the longest days in either one of our long lives.

Chapter Twelve

Since we were the youngest team, we got to stick closer to home in the western part of the US and Canada.

We had done thirty-six of the bastards, then met everyone back in Vegas for dinner and planning. Then we had all gone back out.

It seems our plan was working fine.

But then on number forty-nine, Sims and I ran into a problem.

The moment I went inside the guy's head as he sat at his desk in his office in San Francisco, I knew I wasn't in one of the regular angry wife-beaters.

This guy killed women.

Lots and lots of women and only beat his wife as a hobby, for the most part.

The most evil person I had ever touched.

And I knew where he had buried every one of the poor souls.

I implanted the punch in the balls command deeply, also if he even thought of killing a woman, he would kick a wall as hard as he could for as often as he could until the thought ended.

Then I climbed out and went to find my partner, who had just finished with the wife in their home in the hills of Berkeley.

"She thinks he is a serial killer," Sims said, her face white with shock.

I nodded. "He is. I know where all of them are buried."

"How many?" Sims asked.

"Fifteen here in San Francisco. Another five in college back east."

"I think I'm going to be sick," Sims said.

I agreed with her completely.

We stood there, holding each other.

I have no idea at all how I could have done this job without her beside me.

After a minute we jumped back to the serial killer's office. He lay on the floor behind his desk screaming at his broken ankle and the damage he had done to his groin.

"We need help," I finally said after we stood there for another minute, hand-in-hand, watching the killer roll on the floor in pain. "I honestly have no idea what to do."

Sims nodded.

"Jewel, Tommy, some help?"

A few moments later Jewel and Tommy both appeared next to us. The serial killer was now whimpering on the floor behind his desk, alternating between holding his crotch and his broken foot.

"A serial killer," I said, pointing at the bastard. "Killed twenty. We have no idea what to do."

Jewel and Tommy both nodded.

"We've run into this a few times," Jewel said.

"And you will as well, sadly," Tommy said.

"Take a deep breath, brace yourself, and follow me in there," Tommy said.

I took Sims' hand and we went into the serial killer's body once again.

Tommy quickly showed us how to set a command that for the rest of his life, at any chance, this guy would confess about his crimes and tell anyone who would listen where he buried the bodies.

And in great detail.

It was such an easy solution, I couldn't believe I hadn't thought of it. But I had been so shocked climbing inside the cesspool of serial killer's mind, I just hadn't.

Tommy removed the kicking the wall command I had set and the punching himself in the balls command and replaced them with a command that at any thought of killing or hitting a woman, he would feel extreme remorse. Remorse so intense he would have to tell anyone who would listen what he was feeling and how sorry he was for even thinking it.

And then confess every crime he ever did all over again.

Finally, Tommy planted a command that the killer call the police and report himself and tell them where the bodies were buried.

Then the three of us got out of the sewer of the killer's mind.

It never felt so good to be back in the air.

The killer climbed back into his chair and called the police. As he was saying he had killed some women, he started crying.

Then he started bawling and sobbing like a baby, trying to keep confessing.

"He will not do well in prison," Sims said, shaking her head.

"Exactly," Tommy said, smiling.

With that, Tommy and Jewel left, going back to their list.

I figured that the best thing Sims and I could do was keep going as well and she agreed.

It took us until four in the morning before we finished our list and told Jewel and Tommy and Gail and Sunset.

They were almost done as well. Just a few more each.

All of us looked wiped out.

I felt like I had been dragged through a garbage dump, but I also knew we had saved a lot of lives and punished a lot of abusers in ways the law of live society could never do.

Sims and I got a glass of wine and went out to our deck overlooking the lights of Las Vegas.

We sat in silence, sipping the wine as the cool evening air around us took away some of the memories.

"That was a good day," I said after a few minutes. "I feel like shit, but it was a hell of a good day."

Sims nodded. "Have I ever said how I love how you look at the world?"

"No," I said, smiling at her. "But I'm glad you do because I sure love that wonderful smile and perfect body of yours."

She laughed. "Good, because I was hoping you would be up for scrubbing my back in the shower."

"I would love that," I said. "But only if we can crawl in bed together afterward and just hold each other."

"I'll drink to that," she said, smiling.

We sat drinking for a few more minutes, letting the memories of the monsters we had visited slip from our minds to be replaced by the beautiful view of the lights of the Strip.

Then Sims stood, took my hand, and led me toward the bedroom and a wonderful warm shower that would wash away even more memories of what we had seen in those heads.

We had been faced with a horrid problem. We had found a way to solve it and saved a lot of people in the process.

Ghosts saving lives.

And that felt good, almost as good as getting my back washed by a beautiful woman after a long day.

Almost.

PART THREE

A GHOST FROM THE PAST

CHAPTER THIRTEEN

I had come to love being dead.

Yeah, sounds like the bullet in my forehead actually had scrambled my ghost brains as well as my live ones. Or I had simply gone batty.

I suppose both were a possibility. But I hadn't questioned why I liked being dead until today.

Today started like any other wonderful day since I had died.

I crawled out of Sims' and my massive soft bed right at the crack of noon, went into the kitchen as naked as the day I was born, and got a cup of coffee before heading back to the shower.

Since I was dead, very few people could see me, but I wouldn't have cared. Even dead I didn't look a day over twenty-eight and had never been the shy type.

And since I was dead, I sure didn't plan on aging, so the only thing that would change would be my hair color, something Sims said I changed as fast as the weather.

Of course, we lived in a wonderful condo in Vegas, where the weather didn't change that often, so my gut sense is that my hair was ahead of the weather by a factor of two dozen or so.

Today it was a light blue.

A dead girl has to have a hobby after all.

I was done with my shower and sipping a second cup of coffee and eating a wonderful bagel with cream cheese on our deck when my love showed up and joined me.

Sims kissed me and sat down with a sigh.

The air was getting warm and it felt wonderful against my skin. I had dressed in my normal comfortable jeans, silk blouse, and tennis shoes.

Sims was dressed about the same. And since we were almost exactly the same height and body type, our closets were joint closets. Worked out great that way.

But now this early afternoon I felt great and she was frowning.

She was a morning person and got out to help people while I slept. Then we both worked afternoons together, spent the evenings relaxing together, then I went out and worked evenings on my own while she went off to bed.

So the frown told me she must have had a rough session with someone this morning and the memory wasn't fading fast enough.

What lived in a lot of people's minds could really shock a person. I was still getting shocked almost every day.

The Ghost Agents who trained us, Jewel and Tommy, said they still were shocked sometimes at the ugliness in some people, or the incredible beauty in others.

"Want to talk about it?" I asked, sipping my black coffee and enjoying the view of the Strip.

Sims just shrugged. "Ran into an old friend is all."

"From Boise?" I asked, now turning to face her completely.

Neither of us had talked much about our lives before becoming ghosts. To be honest, it just had never occurred to me.

Sims nodded to my Boise question. "Guy by the name of Stanton, also in banking. He and I had a fling about three months before I died. A really nice guy. Very smart and very sweet."

"Was he good in bed?" I asked, smiling at her and trying to lighten the mood a little.

Sims smiled, clearly in the memory. "Let's just say he did what he needed to do."

"Oh, I like the sounds of that."

She laughed and gave me that seductive wink. "If you're a good girl, I'll tell you every detail later."

"I'm wearing a halo for the rest of the day," I said.

Again she laughed.

"So seeing him got you down?" I asked. "Or did he have something going on with him otherwise?"

Her smile vanished and she nodded. "Not sure what to do."

"Play out what happened for me," I said, reaching across the table and holding her hand. Even in the heat her skin felt cool.

"I saw him down in the MGM Grand lobby early this morning," Sims said. "I almost didn't recognize him. He looked tired, run-down, and clearly depressed. All the signs that Jewel and Tommy taught us to watch for in people who needed help."

I nodded and let her go on.

"So I went to him and inside his head to see what was the problem."

She sat there in silence, the only sounds around us were from the city traffic six flights below.

"And what was the problem?" I asked after a minute.

"My death was the problem," she said.

That sat me back.

"It seems," she said, "he was in love with me. Or thought he was. He was very confused. I thought it just a fling, but after I died it seemed to mean more. He felt like he had lost the love of his life and has been going downhill ever since. But he didn't feel that way before I died."

"Oh, shit," I said softly.

Sims nodded. "He lost his job last week and decided to come to Las Vegas to see if he could get more information from Patty about me and my death, if he could find her. So far he hasn't."

"Oh, shit," I said once again.

If there was ever an "oh shit" moment, this was it.

Sims looked up at me, those wonderful blue eyes drilling right into me as she could do.

"Have you given one thought to the people we knew when we were alive?"

Again that question shocked me.

I hadn't.

Not one thought, not even enough to go see who was at my memorial service, if anyone gave one.

It flat hadn't occurred to me.

Damn it all to hell. Why hadn't I?

"No," I said, staring back into the eyes of the woman I loved. "And that doesn't seem right and doesn't seem like me at all."

"It's not like me either," Sims said. "And I haven't either until this morning. We should have been helping the people like Stanton move on with their lives, not just ignoring them."

"Seems we need some questions answered and then we need to go see some old friends to help them get past our deaths," I said.

Sims nodded. "Starting with Stanton."

"Answers first," I said, not happy in the slightest that maybe someone had brainwashed us in some fashion or another. I wasn't a fan of being controlled in life, I sure wasn't going to be in death.

Sims just nodded.

CHAPTER FOURTEEN

I looked out over the city and said simply, "Jewel, we could use your help for a minute."

Jewel appeared and smiled and sat down at the table on the patio with us. She was taller than Sims and I, but dressed almost exactly the same in a silk blouse, jeans, and tennis shoes. She had her hair pulled back and was smiling when she arrived.

"Ever tell you two how much I love this place you have here?"

Sims and I both smiled.

"We love it as well," Sims said. "Would you like a bagel or some coffee or water?"

Jewel shook her head. "Just finished lunch. Thanks. So what is the problem?"

"You ever think about the people you left behind when you died?" I asked.

Jewel sat back and shook her head, frowning. "At first, no."

"You did after a time?" Sims asked.

"Tommy and I pushed it after about six months," Jewel said. "We thought we had been brainwashed to not care about our old lives or something."

"I'm feeling that exact same way," I said. "It was as if I didn't even give a thought to the impact of my death on people. And if I was brainwashed, I'm not happy about it."

Jewel nodded. "Both Tommy and I were pretty disgusted at ourselves as well."

"So if not brainwashing, what causes it?" Sims asked.

"Death," Jewel said.

I stared at her for a moment, then at the woman I loved.

Sims looked as confused as I felt.

Jewel glanced up and saw our confusion and smiled. "Here is how it was explained to me and Tommy. If you died and didn't become a Ghost Agent, you move into the light and would be able to do nothing for those left behind. Right?"

"But we are Ghost Agents," I said.

Jewel nodded. "But the fact of you dying cleaned out parts of that old life and turned your mind to building a new life."

Sims frowned. "So you mean what happened is a natural part of death?"

"As far as anyone knows," Jewel said. "Yes. Think of it like you have gone from one room to a new room and the door between the rooms closed. Unless you have a specific reason to go back through that door, you don't think about it."

"So there are no rules about us going back and helping people get past our deaths?" I asked.

"None that I have been told," Jewel said. "When Tommy and I came to this same realization, we went back. It wasn't easy, but we think we helped some of our family and friends a little."

Jewel looked at us. "Did something happen?"

Sims nodded. "Ran into an old boyfriend who has let my death almost destroy him."

"Oh," Jewel said. "Looks like you two have a couple of old lives to clean up a little."

I nodded. "Sure seems that way."

"Call if you need help," Jewel said. "And be braced. The emotions and scars you will find in old family and friends will sometimes be tough to deal with. You don't have to do this, you know."

"Yes, we do," I said. "Now that I know what has happened."

Sims nodded.

With that Jewel vanished.

I reached across and held Sims' hand.

"We have each other to get us through this," I said.

She smiled and squeezed my hand. "We do."

"So let's go see if we can help Stanton," I said.

"Ghosts riding to the rescue," she said.

And we both laughed.

Chapter Fifteen

We found Stanton right where Sims had left him an hour before. He was leaning against one of the large marble pillars in the massive MGM Grand Hotel lobby, just sort of staring at nothing.

The sounds of all the people in the lobby was like a dull roar of a river. And through the large archway across the lobby the sounds of laughter and bells from the casino came echoing in clearly.

There had to be a hundred people in the massive, high-ceilinged lobby.

Stanton looked like he had been handsome, something I would not have been surprised about since Sims had dated him. But Sims was right about how he looked now. Tired and clearly not paying attention to his hair or beard.

He looked depressed and lost.

I also would have seen that from a distance.

"He had heard that Patty works the front desk," Sims said, "and is hoping to recognize her from a description I gave him once."

"Does he feel you might have faked your death and are still alive?" I asked.

"He feels I am still around somewhere, but he doesn't know how or why he feels that way. He even tried a couple counseling sessions and they only made things worse."

"Wow, he might have some borderline superpowers of some sort," I said.

"I was thinking the same thing," Sims said. "His sense about me has clearly driven him, just not in a healthy way."

"And we don't know enough yet to be able to show ourselves to live people," I said.

I knew that was an advanced skill we would pick up given time, but we were both so new, that wasn't going to work. We could barely touch something real at the moment. It felt like we were brushing it.

"Don't know if that would help or make it worse for him," Sims said.

"Somehow we have to convince him he is not going insane," I said, "and just needs to remember you, but let go at the same time."

We had been standing near him having that conversation and for some reason he perked up and started looking around, puzzled, as if he had heard us.

Sims noticed that as well.

"Some superheroes can see us," I said. "I'm starting to think Stanton here is a closet superhero."

Sims nodded. "He's approaching thirty. About the time most superheroes start getting their first powers."

I nodded to that. I stopped aging and got my first powers around twenty-eight and so did Sims.

"We need superhero help," I said.

Sims turned and looked out over the crowd. "Patty, if you can hear me, we need a little help in the MGM Grand lobby."

A voice out of nowhere said, "Be right there."

I laughed. "Who knew we could do that?"

Sims laughed as well. "Nice to know, isn't it?"

Poor Stanton just kept staring around, his head moving back and forth like he was watching a tennis match. One thing for certain, we needed to get him out of here before security came and talked to him about being crazy.

At that moment Patty came walking out from behind the MGM front desk and started toward us.

I jumped Sims and me both to a spot beside her and we fell into step with her.

"The guy standing beside the pillar is looking for you," Sims said. "He's an old boyfriend who is feeling broken up about my death and that something is wrong. He has come to talk with you."

"He looks like he is in bad shape," Patty said softly without moving her lips.

"He is," Sims said.

"But he could also sense us standing there beside him," I said. "We think he might be a budding superhero."

"We'll find out," Patty said.

Then Patty said, "Need a little help, partner. Out of time in the lobby around a guy standing near the big pillar I am approaching."

At that moment Stanton saw her walking toward him and smiled.

And with that smile I saw what Sims had seen in him, even for a fling. The guy was hot.

Chapter Sixteen

"**W**hat's his name?" Patty whispered to us as we got close.

"Stanton Henry," Sims said.

Patty extended her hand to Stanton. "Mr. Henry, I understand you were looking for me."

"I was," Stanton said, smiling while looking puzzled as he shook her hand. "But I didn't tell anyone that."

At that moment Poker Boy appeared and the entire lobby froze and all the sound vanished.

"Wow," I said, glancing around. "That's cool."

He smiled. "I kind of think it's cool as well. I just slipped us between a moment in time so we could talk."

Patty was using her superpower to calm Stanton, but he still looked like he might bolt at any moment.

"Think we can learn to do this?" I asked.

Poker Boy shrugged. "Not a clue, but would be fun to find out, wouldn't it?"

"It sure would."

"What's happening?" Stanton managed to say.

Patty let go of Stanton's hand she had been holding at that moment and looked at Sims. "You were right, he is a budding superhero."

"A what?" Stanton asked. "And who are you talking to?"

"Sims," Patty said, turning back to face Stanton.

I could feel that she had her full calming power hitting the poor guy. That much would put an elephant to sleep, and it was calming him, but not by much. He was a strong one.

I could sense Poker Boy add his power to her as he touched Patty's arm and Stanton seemed to calm even more. Those two clearly made a wonderful team.

"Think we need Laverne here to figure out which area he's going to work in?" Poker Boy asked.

At that moment Laverne appeared.

Lady Luck herself, standing there in a power suit with her long hair pulled back tight off her face, giving her a stark, business-woman look.

It fit the most powerful woman in the world as far as I was concerned.

She extended her hand to the shocked Stanton. "My name is Laverne. It is a pleasure to meet you."

He shook her hand and nodded. Clearly with even all the calming power of Patty and Poker Boy, he was too stunned to talk.

Can't say as I blame him. Time stops around him and two people just appear in front of him and call him a superhero. If that would have happened to me like it was happening to him, I would have had myself committed as soon as I woke up.

Or I would have sworn off drinking for a month.

"He's going to be working with Adrian in banking and finance," Laverne said to Poker Boy and Patty.

Then she turned to me, then looked directly at Sims. "You two need to help him get past what he has been feeling since you died."

I nodded. So did Sims.

"I'm going to let him be able to see you," Laverne said. "Take him back to your condo and do what you need to help him get ready to take the next step and get back to work."

Again Sims and I nodded.

"Thank you," Sims said.

At that moment poor Stanton's eyes got wide as suddenly Sims, his dead ex-fling, was standing in front of him.

"Hi, Stanton," Sims said, smiling.

At that, Stanton's eyes sort of rolled up in his head and closed.

I didn't blame him in the slightest. I felt the same way the first time I saw Sims. She was that good-looking.

"Time to move," Poker Boy said.

Poker Boy jumped Stanton and us to our condo, putting the limp Stanton on the couch.

A few minutes later, after Patty could walk back to a dead camera area outside the lobby, she joined us.

"Thanks," Patty said to Poker Boy. "I think we can take it from here."

"Good," he said, kissing his girlfriend on the cheek. "Got a hot ten-twenty no-limit going at the Bellagio."

And he vanished.

Now it was up to the three of us to try to figure out what to do with a very confused, very depressed budding superhero.

I had a hunch we could figure it out.

CHAPTER SEVENTEEN

"We going to need to get into his head first to see if we can help a little before he wakes up?" I asked.

The three of us had moved to chairs in our living room facing the couch. The air-conditioning was keeping the condo at a comfortable temperature, even though the day outside had warmed up into the nineties. Our automatic blinds were blocking the sun on one side of the living room, but letting in enough light that the room was bright and airy.

"I think we should," Sims said, "But I don't think it should be me in there again. At least not just yet."

"I agree," Patty said.

"So do I," I said.

I stood and moved toward the sleeping man. "Back in a

moment. Let me see what I can clean up without changing anything."

I merged inside of Stanton.

Sims was right, since her death he had been majorly conflicted. It seemed what had been a fling to him at the time, when she died, took on more meaning.

I nosed around and discovered that it was his budding superpower that had caused the feeling. He could sense she was still alive, but his rational brain told him otherwise.

And that had set up the conflict.

So I spent about ten minutes just easing his fears, helping him understand a little of what happened, and making him understand that Sims was dead but still around and that he had been right all along.

Just by helping him with those thoughts and blocking some ugly thoughts of hopelessness, I could sense he was feeling better. He had a solid core of good and was clearly a very nice person.

Finally I suggested he wake up and I left him and went back to my chair.

"He's going to need more work," I said to the worried look on my partner. "But I think in the long run he's going to be fine. He's a really solid and nice guy."

She nodded as Stanton slowly came awake and then looked around. Finally he sat up.

"Was that a dream in the lobby? Am I still dreaming this?"

"Not a dream," Sims said.

Sims pointed to me. "This is my partner and lover, Marble Grant. Marble is another Ghost Agent like I am."

Then Sims indicated Patty. "This is our good friend Patty Ledgerwood. She is a superhero as both Marble and I used to be."

"Superhero?" Stanton asked.

"We'll explain everything," Sims said, smiling. "I promise."

"But you died, didn't you?" Stanton asked.

"I did," Sims said. "Just outside of Vegas in a motorcycle accident."

"And remember the shooting in Boise in the alley about eight months ago where two people were killed?" I asked.

Stanton looked at me. "The real estate agent and her date?"

"That was me," I said, smiling.

He just shook his head and looked at his hands in his lap. "Horrid dream."

I laughed, which surprised him and he looked up.

"Take a look at this view," I said, sweeping my arms in the direction of the city. "Take a look at this fantastic city out there and this amazing condo you are sitting in. Nothing at all horrid about any of it. And you have three people here trying to help you, so that's not so bad either."

"Help me do what?" he asked.

"You came looking for Patty and you found her," Sims said. "You felt there was something more to my death, you sensed it, and you were right, but that conflict tore you apart. Am I right?"

He nodded.

"So now you have found out what happened to me. I am here and working as a Ghost Agent. And because you will soon be getting training as a superhero as well, you can see me."

"I'm no superhero," he said, shaking his head. "I can't even keep a job."

"Because you knew something was different with Sims and the transformation you are going through," I said. "A perfect storm you will soon get under control if you let us help you."

After a moment he did as I thought he would. He nodded.

He was one strong person.

"Good," Patty said, checking her watch. "I got to get to work. Call me or Poker Boy if you need help."

"We'll be fine," Sims said, smiling at Stanton.

Patty nodded and vanished.

"What the hell?" he asked.

"Given some time," I said, smiling at the handsome man sitting on our couch, "you might be able to do that as well."

"She's right," Sims said. "But right now we have a problem."

"What's that?" I asked my wonderful partner.

"He's alive, we're dead. How in the world are we going to get lunch?"

Then it dawned on us both at the same time.

"Take out!"

CHAPTER EIGHTEEN

O ver the next few days Stanton slowly got used to living with two women ghosts.

We had a spare bed in our second bedroom and he brought his suitcase from his small hotel to the condo.

After a while the questions he asked were one right after another, some of which we had to call in either Patty or Jewel to help answer.

Having him here actually helped Sims and me learn a lot more about our own place in things. He asked questions we might not have thought of asking for years to come.

I was slowly coming to the conclusion that Stanton was frighteningly smart, much smarter than I had thought when in his head trying to dig through all the confusion.

Twice during the two days he was visited by Adrian, a blonde woman who was the god of finance and banking. Both times they went out onto the patio and talked and both times Stanton came back in smiling. It seemed he really liked his new boss. They clearly spoke the same language.

It seemed that as he got to accept the craziness of suddenly being a superhero, he was taking to it quickly. A lot faster than I had done as I slowly grew into my superhero powers.

Of course I didn't have an entire group of people willing to answer questions at the drop of a hat either. I went decades with more questions than answers.

It was on the third day he was there that I forgot about him and staggered out of bed at my normal crack of noon and headed for the kitchen, nude as a baby for my first cup of coffee.

"Now I see why you love her so much," Stanton said from the dining room table.

I glanced over where he and Sims were both smiling at me.

"Yeah," Sims said. "She's hot in a lot of ways."

"No talking in the morning," I mumbled, grabbed my coffee and headed back toward the bedroom.

"Nice ass," Sims said from the dining room.

Stanton just laughed.

And that made me smile. It seemed we had saved one. He said he planned on leaving in a few days to go back to Boise and go back to work.

I was honestly going to miss him. He was such a good guy with a big heart.

But it would be nice to just be back to me and Sims again.

Two days later, the night before he was to leave, Sims

rolled over in bed and said softly, "Think Stanton is healthy enough for a three-way with two ghosts?"

I laughed. "Is that even possible?"

She smiled at me that wonderful smile I had come to love in a very short time. "We're learning to touch physical things."

"I'm all the way up to brushing something lightly," I said. Then I laughed. "You know, that might just be enough."

"Exactly what I was thinking," Sims said. "And as we get better at touching things over the years, he could always come back for more tests."

"He's a test subject?" I asked, laughing.

"Think he'll mind?"

"From what I saw in his mind," I said, "he's completely heterosexual. I doubt if he's ever had a fantasy about two ghost women, but I know he's thought of two women."

"You up for it?" Sims asked.

"Oh, heavens, yes," I said. "As long as you are with me."

A minute later, as Sims and I crawled into his bed totally naked, Stanton asked if he was dreaming again. He then shuddered and moaned as Sims touched him lightly as an answer.

As I have said over and over since I died, being dead is a ton more fun than being alive.

And for the next two hours with Stanton and Sims, I proved that to myself many times over.

Part Four

A New Partner

CHAPTER NINETEEN

Sims and I called Wednesday "Heart Day."

After about three months of being a Ghost Agent team, tasked to help as many people as we could with just about everything, we had decided to make one day a focus on heart attacks.

Wednesday.

Sims and I both loved Wednesdays. Well, actually, we both loved just about any day since we had died, but for some reason, because we had given Wednesday a name, it had become sort of special.

The night before I had tinted my long hair a slightly different color blue for the day and Sims had done her toenails in bright blue. She even let me blow on her toenails to help them dry, which had sent shivers down her back followed by a fit of giggling when I wouldn't stop blowing and a quick trip to our wonderful large bed for far more than just giggling.

One thing I could say about sex while dead. It was a whole lot better than when I was alive, and I thought it pretty good back then. It also might be better because I was head-over-tennis-shoes in love with my beautiful and smart partner and her wonderful trim body.

We had decided last night to start off this Wednesday out on the Strip in front of the MGM Grand Hotel. I had on my normal outfit of jeans, tennis shoes, and silk blouse. Today, because it was supposed to be a hot fall afternoon, I decided to not wear a bra, which gave Sims a look at my nipples through my blouse anytime she wanted.

I had my off-blue long hair pulled back and large dangling earrings.

Sims dressed exactly the same except she had on a bra and had her blonde hair pulled back and up on the back of her head to keep her neck cool. And she had only stud earrings.

Ghost Agents felt heat and cold just like anyone did. Maybe even a little more intensely since food tasted more intense and sex felt more intense. Seemed like being a ghost just heightened every sensation.

When we arrived on the hot, wide sidewalk on the Strip, both carrying tall water bottles, it was already full of tourists, most walking slowly in the already warm desert air.

The point of our Heart Day was to find people who were on the verge of having a heart attack and get them help in the local hospital. One of the ghosts who had trained us, Jewel, had been a medical doctor when alive. She had shown us how to go into a person and look for exact signs of a coming heart attack.

Sometimes, if the heart attack was only a distant threat, we planted thoughts in the person's head to get checked up when they got home. But at times, with that kind of focus on looking for one thing, we had actually found a few over the last couple of months we literally had to rush to a hospital. More than likely we had saved their lives and that felt great, to be honest.

"So where do we start today?" Sims asked, looking at the people passing by.

As Jewel had told us, it was impossible to tell a possible heart attack candidate from the physical appearance alone. Extreme weight, difficulty breathing often meant problems with many other things such as diabetes and cancer. If too many things were wrong like that, Sims and I had decided to just plant suggestions to eat less, exercise more, and get to a doctor as soon as the person got home.

Jewel had showed us how to make that suggestion like a nasty itch that needed to be scratched more and more the longer the person waited.

I had lost count of how many heavy people I had seen who were not going to a doctor and who I put that itch need in their minds. I just hoped Jewel was right and it worked. She said it did.

At that moment, I spotted a really handsome man, in his

mid-thirties, with dark hair, intense dark eyes, and an expensive suit walking toward us. He had no tie on under the suit jacket and his shirt was open two buttons.

He made the day instantly hotter.

The guy walked like he owned the world and was paying no attention to his surroundings or the tourists, so more than likely he was a local.

"You looking at what I am looking at?" Sims asked.

"Trying not to melt," I said.

She laughed and said, "What do you say we climb inside for a ride to cool down."

I just laughed with her, fairly convinced that climbing inside this guy wasn't going to do anything to cool either of us down. It was as if he had walked off the pages of *GQ Magazine*.

As he strode past, both Sims and I melted inside the handsome man.

And then we both started laughing. Not only was he handsome on the outside, this guy was like the perfect man and a superhero to boot.

His name, and I do not kid, was Canyon Stevens.

He was a superhero in the area of sales and business and worked as a high-paying manager of sales of one of the major casino chains. He had been a superhero for only about fifteen years and still didn't have a lot of his powers.

He wasn't even that sure of the ones he did have. They just seemed like normal stuff to him.

I had never heard of the God of Sales that he worked for

in the superhero world. There was a lot I didn't know about superheroes and gods and who even ran all us Ghost Agents.

Canyon loved women, but at the moment he had no girl-friend or wife because he was too busy funding and helping three different start-up businesses around town as well as doing his own job. His start-ups helped get jobs for those in need and helped train others in new tech work.

Could this guy get any better?

He lived alone in a nice condo just off the Strip and kept it clean. He had no real vices other than he liked to drink a little too much at times.

I liked to drink like that as well. So did Sims. Even as ghosts we had been known to toss back a few too many.

And that was his only vice.

"This is what our minds would have looked like to a ghost coming in," Sims said.

"Squeaky clean do-gooders," I said.

"Overachievers," Sims said.

"Yeah, that too," I said, laughing.

Canyon had turned and was heading up the sidewalk toward the MGM Hotel lobby. He had a business meeting in an expensive restaurant there, but he stopped suddenly and looked around as if someone was following him.

"Oh, oh," I said. "He senses us."

"Wow," Sims said. "He's pretty good."

At that we both shut up and after a second Canyon shook his head, wondering what he had heard, and headed into the front lobby of the hotel.

The high-ceilinged place was noisy and had a good hundred people milling around. Huge marble pillars separated the area with people's luggage stacked against the pillars in places.

Patty Ledgerwood, aka Front Desk Girl, was standing behind the long wooden check-in desk of the MGM Grand registration. She looked up, beamed and waved at Canyon, who waved back as he headed across the lobby.

He knew her and was happy to see her. He did not know she was Poker Boy's girlfriend, just that she was a superhero and very nice. But he wasn't attracted to her. He liked his women more like what Sims and I looked like. Tallish, thin, long hair, and a love of sex.

Damn, too bad he was alive and we were dead. Sims and I could have had a blast with him.

"Well, we probably had better drop off this joyride and get to work," Sims said.

"We haven't checked his heart yet," I said, not really wanting to leave Canyon just yet. It wasn't often we got to ride along in a mind that was so clear and without issues.

"Good point," Sims said, laughing.

Again Canyon stopped and looked around.

Sims and I did what Jewel had taught us to do and focused in on the pumping heart of Canyon. It looked fine, no sign at all of heart problems that I could see.

"What the hell is that?" Sims asked.

I looked closer and saw what she was looking at.

A bubble of some sort, or a growth, seemed to have

expanded off the back of Canyon's heart. It did not look healthy in any fashion.

In fact, it looked like it might explode with any heartbeat.

Shit, just shit.

CHAPTER TWENTY

C anyon was waiting with a few tourists now to get on an elevator to take him to the restaurant for his meeting. He knew he was hearing voices, but he couldn't figure out from where.

Or why.

It didn't have him panicked, just puzzled.

The man was about as calm as they came.

"Get Jewel," I said to Sims. "I'll stop him from getting on this elevator."

"Why stop me?" Canyon said out loud.

Sims vanished and I felt stunned that Canyon could hear me that clearly.

A couple of the tourists just looked at him and Canyon covered nicely by pointing at his ear as if talking on a phone they couldn't see.

"Just move away from the elevator and hold on," I said as clear as I could to Canyon. "My name is Marble Grant and I'm a Ghost Agent who used to be a superhero like you."

Canyon just shook his head, but moved away from the elevator and out of the traffic pattern.

A moment later Jewel appeared and she and Sims joined me inside of Canyon.

"He can hear us clearly," I said to them.

"Yes, I can," he said out loud.

"Back right there," Sims said to Jewel.

Jewel took one look at the problem and said simply, "Shit."

"Well, that doesn't sound promising," Canyon said, "for whatever you are doing."

"Hang tight," I said to Canyon.

We all stepped outside of Canyon and stood beside him.

Jewel was about our height and dressed almost identically as Sims and me. And she looked as worried as I had ever seen her look.

"He needs a hospital right now and emergency surgery," Jewel said. "I doubt he's going to make it through the day or even to the hospital."

"You're kidding me?" Sims asked, looking over at the handsome and healthy superhero standing beside us looking puzzled.

Even puzzled, Canyon's square jaw and dark, intense eyes made him drop-dead handsome. But it seemed that Mr. Perfect wasn't so perfect after all.

And if we didn't do something quick, dropping dead would be exactly what Mr. Perfect would be doing. I trusted Jewel completely on that diagnosis.

"He can't jump and we can't jump him," Sims said.

I knew what we needed to do. "He needs to get to Patty and she will jump him to the hospital. She's at the front desk right now."

Jewel nodded. "Marble, you get him to Patty. Sims, you come with me and we'll get the hospital staff prepared that he is coming and what to look for."

"I'll shout when Patty and I have him ready to jump," I said.

"I'll find a safe place to jump him in the hospital," Sims said.

They both vanished and I stepped back into Canyon's body.

"I'm back," I said as clearly as I could. "You need to go talk with Patty at the front desk right now."

"Why?" he asked.

"I can make you do it," I said. "But I don't want to. More than enough time for answers on the way. Just get going."

He seemed annoyed, but he turned and headed back toward the lobby.

I decided to not sugarcoat the facts. He seemed like the type that could handle bad news.

"You have on your heart what looks like a large bubble that is about to break," I said. "Two other Ghost Agents are at the hospital right now getting them ready for you, but we need Patty to jump you there. We do not believe you would survive the cab ride."

I was impressed. He heard every word I said and only panicked a little.

I think if I had a voice in my head telling me I was on the verge of dying, I might be screaming and running in circles with my hands over my head shouting that the body snatchers were invading.

I hoped I wouldn't do that, but fairly certain I would have.

Canyon's worry at what I had said sent his heart rate up, which scared me more than it did him I'm sure.

"How did you figure this out?" he asked out loud.

"Accident," I said. "We'll explain after we get this fixed. Right now I have to leave you to talk with Patty. Just stand and smile at her."

He stopped in front of the long check-in desk of the hotel as I left his body.

Patty was surprised to see me appear like that suddenly out of the side of Canyon.

I walked through the desk and got close to her as she waited on a live person with two kids trying to check in.

"Canyon there has a bubble about to explode on his heart," I said. "Going to kill him at any moment. Jewel and Sims are at the hospital getting doctors ready. Can you jump him to Sims?"

Patty pretended to cover her ear as if talking on a headpiece, then said, "Yes, I can do that. In the hall to the right behind the counter."

I went back to Canyon and slipped back inside him, something I had to admit I was enjoying. And would enjoy as long as he kept living.

"We go through the door in the counter to the right and into the hallway beyond," I told him.

He looked at Patty and she nodded as she got another person to take over what she was doing for the couple.

"She can see you?"

"If I'm outside of you," I said, "yes she can."

Without me giving much direction, he got buzzed through the door in the counter and with Patty at his side the three of us went down the hallway.

"Sims, we're coming," I said out loud to my partner.

"I'm in a no-person, no-camera area," I heard Sims' voice say. "I'll jump back and direct Patty."

An instant later Sims appeared next to Patty.

"Can I give you where to jump to?" Sims asked her.

"Please," Patty said.

I stayed inside Canyon and watched as Sims touched Patty's arm.

Patty nodded and a moment later all of us were in a corridor in the hospital.

"Thanks, Patty," Sims said.

"Good luck," Patty said to Canyon. "You are in the best hands possible."

With that she jumped back to work.

Canyon was now feeling very worried, but focused on moving forward. He really was a superhero considering that at this very moment he was supposed to be eating lunch with a client.

Five very short minutes later I was standing beside Sims out of Canyon after giving him some help calming down and reminding him to call his lunch date and apologize.

Jewel was inside one of the heart surgeons, doing quick tests on Canyon and getting emergency images of Canyon's heart, telling the woman where to look and what to look for.

Less than one hour later they wheeled Canyon into surgery.

Not a damn thing we could do at that point but wait.

Jewel stayed in the doctor's head for the surgery and we jumped to the MGM Grand to tell Patty that Canyon was in surgery.

Then we jumped back to our condo to get lunch and wait for news.

I hate waiting.

Sims seemed to hate it as much as I did.

CHAPTER TWENTY-ONE

J ust over two hours after they wheeled Canyon into the operating room, Jewel called us and we jumped back to her side in the hospital.

We were standing in a recovery room and Canyon was in a bed covered with a sheet and more tubes and tape than I could imagine having stuck in and on one human body. All around him machines were working showing stuff I had no clue as to meaning.

Two nurses hovered over him.

All I knew was that Jewel was smiling.

"You two saved his life," she said. "That was a hereditary problem that if you hadn't caught would have burst and killed him almost instantly at any point."

Heart Day just got better.

I hugged Sims and she hugged me back.

"He's going to need a bunch of care once he gets out of here," Jewel said. "You two up for the task, since he has no family?"

I was shocked. "Us?"

"Never imagined myself as Nancy Nurse," Sims said, glancing at the covered body of Canyon.

"I can find you the costume I am sure," I said. "It would be sexy on you."

Jewel and Sims both laughed and Sims hugged me again.

"I think I can get Laverne to allow him to see us," Jewel said. "I'll help you and check in on him as well as his human doctors will."

"We do have a spare bedroom," I said, smiling at my partner.

"I am sure Patty can get Poker Boy to put a hospital bed in there for a short time," Jewel said.

"How long are we talking?" Sims asked a moment before I could.

Jewel shrugged. "He will be out of here in about six days from the looks of how healthy he is other than that bubble. He will need about three weeks, maybe a month of watching and care before he should go back to living alone."

"We would need a live person to cook some meals," I said.

"I have a hunch that Madge on Poker Boy's team might be willing to help with that," Jewel said, "and jump the meals to your place until he can cook himself."

I looked into the wonderful blue eyes of my partner and smiled. "You up for it?"

She nodded. "Something new and he is damn nice to look at, you have to admit."

"He is at that," I said. "Especially after he gets healthy again."

So six days later, with Jewel watching carefully, we helped Poker Boy and Patty and Madge get Canyon into our apartment.

It turned out that except for a few issues in the first few days, Canyon was a perfect patient. He did as instructed and let the two of us boss him around.

For the first week, either Sims or I were always there with him. But after that we went back to pretty much our normal routine. And it was on the Wednesday morning, three weeks after we saved Canyon's life, that I went a little too much back to our old routine.

My habit in the morning, before Canyon moved in, was to crawl out of bed stark naked, go into the kitchen where Sims had a cup of coffee waiting for me, take the coffee and go back to the bathroom and shower.

As I reached the kitchen, still mostly sound asleep, I heard a wolf-whistle from Sims who was sitting at the kitchen table.

And beside her was a very healthy-looking Canyon, smiling.

Damn, that was the second time I had done that in front of a guest. I really needed to wake up just a touch in the morning.

"Don't get any ideas, mister," I said to his smile. "You ain't healthy enough to handle this yet."

With that I toasted them with my coffee mug and turned and headed for the bathroom as they both laughed.

And from that moment on the three of us were fine.

We became not only friends, but roommates.

Canyon started cooking and we learned that not only was he good for the eye, he knew how to cook some amazing meals. He said he had almost stopped cooking because he hated cooking only for himself. He loved cooking for us because he only made enough for just himself, but all three of us could eat.

And as he got feeling better, his true sense of humor and dry wit came out. And his fantastic intelligence. He could see things with people that both Sims and I would miss.

When he left, I was not only going to miss him as a friend, I was going to miss his sense of humor, his calmness, his incredible good looks, and his fantastic cooking.

When Jewel finally gave Canyon the all-clear to go back to his condo after three weeks, both Sims and I just sort of moped around.

I mean, I hadn't been that depressed in a long time, and Sims said she felt the same way.

We talked about drinking, but that felt like a little too much work.

Our wonderful condo now felt empty.

So we talked about it and we both decided that Canyon, if he wanted, could be part of our team, move back in, and the three of us do what we could to help people.

The idea made us both happy again. But I was really worried that he would turn us down.

After all, he had lived with two mostly-crazy ghost women for three weeks.

So instead of worrying about it all night, we went to his place and actually rang his doorbell, something that took both of us to do, and a lot of willpower. We were still not that good at touching and moving real things.

Canyon was surprised to see us standing there in the hall looking worried.

But his smile was genuine.

So he asked us in and we just stood there inside his condo door and blurted out what we were thinking like two school-girls afraid we would get turned down.

And as we talked, Canyon's grin got bigger.

"Two new superhero Ghost Agents and a new superhero business guy teaming up?" he asked.

I nodded. "Pretty much."

"Strangest team in all the land, that would be for sure," Sims said.

"Who knows what we could accomplish," he said, smiling.

"Who knows what could go wrong," Sims said, laughing.

I knew right then that we had him.

"If you say yes," I said, "would you agree to cook at times?"

He laughed and said simply, "I would love to."

"And wear an apron without pants?" Sims asked.

He smiled and looked at Sims, then at me. "Maybe."

"Damn," I said, grasping my chest, "now I'm having a heart attack."

They both laughed.

And with that he got us all drinks and we toasted the formation of our new team.

And the fun we were going to have.

Oh, boy, were we going to have fun.

PART FIVE

FIRST MISSION

CHAPTER TWENTY-TWO

Two months after we joined together to form our new team, Canyon was making our two-bedroom condo a slice of heaven with the smells from his fantastic cooking.

Both Sims and I had started making it a habit to sit at the kitchen counter. We would just sit there and talk and watch Canyon cook.

It was like a dance of beauty as far as we were concerned.

And his sense of humor kept us all laughing at the same time.

Another real nice thing about having him there was that he was alive and could touch things and move them. Until Canyon moved in with us, we had a wonderful living area of soft couches and chairs with a television on the wall that we seldom turned on because it was just far too much work.

Neither one of us was real good at pushing a button on a remote. How sad was that?

Not a great deal annoyed us about being dead, but that one detail did and we worked on it all the time. Both Sims and I really needed to learn how to touch real physical things, make them move just a little. Not only would it come in handy at times when we were trying to save someone, but for real-life-things like turning on a light switch or a television.

But since we had both been dead a very short time, we were told by Jewel that the touching skill was still in our future.

Now, on normal days, I was the last person awake of our little team of superheroes and ghosts. Canyon was always gone, off at work in his expensive, tailored suits, when I came staggering out of bed to get my coffee.

And Sims would have gone out on her own a few times as well. Once I got my sorry ass moving, Sims and I then worked together in the afternoon and early evening. Then we would spend time at home together with Canyon for dinner. Then after both Canyon and Sims were off to bed, I headed out for a late-night patrol.

This morning, expecting no one to be in the kitchen when I came staggering out, I was surprised to see both Sims and Canyon sitting at the kitchen counter sipping coffee.

And neither of them had on their happy face.

But wow did the kitchen smell wonderful of coffee, maybe the richest smell I had had the pleasure to experience. Usually Sims just brought me a cup of coffee from a nearby coffee shop. But this morning Canyon had brewed some fresh.

I had started wearing a bathrobe to the kitchen for my pre-shower coffee after Canyon moved in, so as I poured a cup, I said, "I suppose I really shouldn't ask."

"Get your shower and your coffee," Sims said. "Then we'll talk over your breakfast and our lunches."

Canyon nodded. "We ran into a situation that will take all three of us to deal with."

That was a first. I nodded and turned to head back to the bedroom with my coffee mug in my hand. As I went, I took a sip.

And damn near had an orgasm right there at the edge of the kitchen.

The coffee was rich, had a flavor I couldn't identify, but didn't mind, and just sort of went into my system like a shot of drugs.

Now I know that things taste better when you are dead, but I don't think my heart could handle coffee tasting this good every morning.

I turned and looked back at both Sims and Canyon who were still not smiling.

"What the hell is this?" I asked, pointing at my mug.

"Incredible coffee, isn't it?" Sims asked, picking up her mug.

"By far the best I have ever tasted," I said. "Where did you find it?"

Canyon frowned. And even with a frown he was still the most handsome man a girl could dream about.

"That's the problem we need to talk about," he said.

Great, just great.

The problem was the best-tasting coffee I could have ever imagined drinking. It was going to be one of those days in heaven.

Chapter Twenty-Three

I finished my amazing mug of coffee and my shower in record time and was back in the kitchen with Sims and Canyon before Canyon had a sandwich made and some eggs and toast cooking for me.

Canyon was wearing his dress shirt and slacks and had his suit coat tossed over the back of a bar stool at the counter. Sims wore the same basic thing she and I wore every day. Tennis shoes, jeans, and expensive blouses. Since we were ghosts, we could see no reason to dress up for going out to work since no one could see us anyway.

Canyon made one sandwich for himself and Sims ate the ghost element of his sandwich. It didn't bother the flavor for him at all. The eggs and toast and bacon I was eating would get tossed out in the real world because all I would do would be to eat the ghost element of them.

However, Canyon said he would save the bacon for sandwiches later.

I noticed that neither Sims nor Canyon were drinking coffee when I arrived and the coffee pot was empty and turned upside down in the sink to be rinsed out later.

We all took our food to the dining room table and as we all started eating, I slowly managed to dig my brain out of the last dream I had been having when I woke up.

Finally, I asked, "What was that coffee thing all about?"

"This morning," Canyon said, "I was meeting with a young couple about a start-up they were trying to put together. They wanted to expand their small coffee shop out near the old Bolder Highway into a chain of shops."

"Seems a little small-fry for the types of things you normally deal with," I said to Canyon.

Canyon nodded. "I look at all levels, usually above this sort of thing, but I was asked by a friend of theirs to look at what they were planning and see if I could maybe get them to the right level of funding."

"They have a decent plan?" Sims asked between bites of the BLT sandwich.

"They did, actually," Canyon said, nodding. "Some basic beginner issues, but their plan was solid and their income on their small first store showed the potential."

"So what went wrong?" I asked.

"While I had them filling out some forms for me," he said, "I looked up their location and some pictures of their place. A normal small coffee shop should not be doing those sorts of income numbers. So I dug deeper and found that every picture and article showed lines of cars down the block for their drive-up and half-block lines for their walk-up window."

"I can believe it," I said, remembering that cup of coffee and how it tasted. It felt almost addictive.

"You guys have those little alarm bells in your head when something feels wrong?" Canyon asked.

"I call it my little voice," Sims said, nodding.

"Mine actually sounds like a bell on a small store door," I said, "which I have to admit is a ton better than say a Star Trek door-swoosh opening sound."

Canyon laughed and Sims smiled.

"I hear that swoosh sound every time I kiss you," Sims said to me. "I am pretty sure it's the sound of my panties falling off."

Canyon, bless his heart, blushed, and I just laughed.

"So you had alarm bells go off," Sims said. "So what did you do?"

"I said to the couple that I was interested in helping them, but would need to see their place and sample their coffee."

"And that's when you sampled their coffee and brought some home for us?" I asked.

Canyon nodded. "The moment I tasted it I knew it was too good to be true. But I honestly have no experience in this sort of thing."

"We need to go find out what they are doing," I said to Sims.

"Give us the address," Sims said to Canyon as we stood and both pushed our plates in.

Canyon gave us the address. I knew exactly where it was.

"What do the young owners look like?" Sims said.

Canyon gave us a quick description and said they should either be there or at their small office in a nearby warehouse.

"We'll be right back," I said.

I sure hoped that this coffee was real and legitimate. But the little warning bell in my head was telling me it wasn't going to be.

And that we needed to be damn careful.

Chapter Twenty-Four

Only four young college-aged kids were working in the roadside coffee shop. It was the size of a small bedroom inside and smelled so thick of coffee I bet you could almost drink the air.

All four of the college kids were efficient and friendly and had no idea about anything other than getting tips and getting as many people through the lines as they could. We checked all of them out quickly and then jumped to the office in the warehouse.

Only the young couple was there.

The office was small and stark, with a room behind the office that functioned as a supply warehouse for their one shop. There were two metal desks, a computer on each, one window beside the door, and tile on the floor. The lighting was hanging florescent. I felt more like I had stepped into a prison than an office.

The woman was working on an accounting program on a computer and the guy was on the phone with a supplier of some sort.

Both of them looked like any young late-twenties couple. He had short hair, she had medium black hair, and both wore dressy clothes that were not expensive, clearly still on from having their meeting with Canyon. They both wore matching wedding rings and both looked intent.

"The guy first?" I said. "Let's go in together and be careful?"

Sims nodded. "Something feels very off here and damned if I can spot it."

"Feeling the same way," I said.

I took her hand and we stepped into the guy sitting at the desk.

And it was like sinking into a black pool of ink.

No thoughts, just pure blackness.

Evil blackness.

I yanked Sims sideways and we tumbled to the ground beside the guy.

We both lay on the dirty tile of the office floor, panting, staring up at the guy as he went on with his phone call as if nothing was wrong.

Then it finally dawned on me what I was seeing.

The guy's aura was almost black. So was the woman's aura.

"No aura," I said to Sims as I tried to catch my breath.

She nodded.

When we had trained, we had learned to look at people's auras to get a sense if they needed help or not. Everyone had colorful auras and we had used the training to just sort of link in with our gut sense.

No wonder we thought something was wrong here. We didn't even notice that both of them had almost no aura. And that what they had was black.

"Back to the condo," I said.

Sims nodded and a moment later we were standing beside Canyon in our wonderful kitchen, breathing hard.

We needed help and we needed it quickly.

"Jewel, emergency."

Jewel was one of the Ghost Agents who had trained us. Jewel had been a medical doctor when alive and she was the one who taught us to look for heart problems in people that had then saved Canyon's life.

Jewel appeared, looking worried.

Canyon was also looking worried at our reaction.

"What does it mean when someone has nothing but a slight black aura?" Sims asked a half-second before I could.

"And inside them is pure blackness," I said. "No thoughts, nothing."

"How long were you in there?" Jewel demanded.

"A second, maybe two," I said.

She nodded. "I'm coming in."

She stepped inside me and I could feel a wave of slight heat wash through my body.

Then she stepped out and did the same for Sims.

"You are both clear," Jewel said after she stepped out of Sims. "No infections and I put up a shield just in case I missed something."

"Infection?" Sims asked before I could get the word out of my panicked brain.

Jewel nodded. "You just came in contact with pure evil. That blackness, once spread, could take you over completely."

"So that's what happened to those two people?" Canyon asked.

"You touched them?" Jewel asked, turning to Canyon.

"Shook their hands," he said.

"I'm coming in," Jewel said.

She disappeared inside of Canyon, then came back out a moment later, nodding. "You were also clear and I gave you a protection as well."

Canyon's handsome face looked white and he nodded his thanks.

"So tell us how you found these people," Jewel said, pulling out a chair at the dining room table and sitting.

I sure wished I could move a real chair like that.

Sims and I sat in our normal chairs that were already pulled out and Canyon took his normal chair.

And for the next ten minutes we carefully relayed to Jewel everything that had happened for the three of us this morning.

Including drinking the coffee.

After we were done Jewel sort of looked at something above her for a moment and then nodded. "Magic. Magic that has already gone black."

I didn't even know magic existed until that moment, let alone that it could go black.

But I sure didn't like the sounds of it in the slightest.

Sims took my hand and squeezed it. Clearly she didn't much like it either.

CHAPTER TWENTY-FIVE

Jewel spent the next fifteen minutes explaining to us that what seems like magic that superheroes and gods do is actually just talents we all have. And that we practice and improve on like practicing music.

But actual magic does exist in the world and when used, almost always turns black fairly quickly and corrupts the user. There is no such thing as good magic.

"So the coffee beans are magical?" I asked. "That's why they taste so good?"

"I would bet that was the case," Jewel said. "More than likely this young couple picked up this magic skill at some point to help their business. And when magic is used for selfish purposes like that, it turns black even faster."

"What about all the people drinking it?" Sims asked. "Are they contaminated now?"

"No," Jewel said, shaking her head. "Thankfully it doesn't work that way. But we will have to check back on all of the couple's suppliers and their workers."

"I have all their records at my office," Canyon said. "They were very complete in trying to get the financing."

"Good," Jewel said.

"So what do we do now to stop this?" I asked, almost afraid of the answer. I really never wanted to get near anything that black again.

Jewel just shook her head. "Cleaning out this kind of thing is way above all of us. Now it's time to bring in the big guns. The use of magic is one of the worst crimes in all of the world. And there are entire forces of gods and superheroes who have the task of just containing and stopping the use of magic. Our job is to find it. Nothing more."

Both Sims and I nodded.

I felt relieved, more than I wanted to admit.

Jewel looked upward slightly and focused. "Laverne, we have a magic problem."

A moment later the most powerful god in all the world appeared.

Canyon scrambled to his feet and Jewel and Sims and I also stood, but a little more calmly. We had been around Laverne, Lady Luck herself, a few times already. Canyon had as well, but only once after his operation.

Laverne had on a power suit that fit her trim frame perfectly. She had her dark brown hair pulled back tightly off her face that gave her a stark look.

"Magic?" Laverne asked Jewel.

"A pretty bad infestation," Jewel said, nodding. "These three found it this morning."

Laverne looked at Sims and me and then at poor Canyon who looked like he might faint at any moment. As a new superhero, you just never imagined you would ever face the most powerful god of them all.

"You make sure they are clean?" Laverne asked.

"I did," Jewel said. "But would not hurt for you to do so as well in case I missed something.

Laverne nodded and sort of waved her hand at the three of us standing beside the table. Again I felt a wave of heat pass through me. I imagined that would be what a hot flash would feel like, but knew I would never get that personal hell since I had died and my periods stopped cold.

As I said, being dead was like living in heaven.

"They are clean," Laverne said. "Now, we need to get started cleaning out the infection."

"It is the owners of a small coffee shop down off the old Boulder Highway," Jewel said. "They did something to make their coffee taste better."

"I have all the information about who they are, their suppliers, and so on in a file at my office."

"Good job, everyone," Laverne said. "Canyon, come with me for the file and I'll get it to the right team to clean it all up."

Canyon and Laverne vanished at that moment.

"Very good job you two," Jewel said, smiling at me and Sims. "But next time, if you see a black aura, don't go near it."

"Oh, trust me, we won't," I said.

"I don't even think I'll ever drink coffee again," Sims said.

Jewel laughed. "No need to go that far."

"Oh, good," Sims said.

Jewel laughed and then vanished.

Sims and I slumped back into our chairs at the dining room table.

"We got lucky," I said.

Sims nodded. "That could have been so, so much worse."

At that moment Canyon appeared back at the dining room table and also slumped into a chair. His face was pure white and he looked like he had just had a near-death experience.

"Lady Luck thanked me and smiled at me," he said, his voice like a small child opening a wonderful gift on Christmas.

"Fantastic," I said.

Sims agreed and we just kept smiling at our shaken superhero.

Finally Canyon took a deep breath and looked up. "And then Lady Luck said I needed to start practicing jumping from one place to the next if I was going to work with and try to keep up with you two."

"You can teleport?" Sims asked.

I was stunned. If he could that would be such good news.

"I think so," Canyon said, nodding.

"Into your bedroom," I said. "Now. Don't think about it. Just jump there."

He vanished and both Sims and I started applauding.

He appeared a second later, grinning from ear to ear.

"It seems Lady Luck likes the idea of our little team," I said.

"She really does," Canyon said.

"This deserves a celebration," Sims said, clapping her hands together and laughing.

"I think what I need is a drink," Canyon said. "Maybe two."

So out we went drinking and then dancing.

Lots of dancing, lots of drinking.

The three of us dancing was so much fun. I had no idea that dancing after death was so much fun.

Celebrating our team and our first really major win felt right.

And as the evening went on, only a few people looked oddly at the handsome man in the silk suit laughing and dancing alone on the dance floor.

After all, it was Vegas and things like that happened in Vegas.

Besides, we were there with him. He was far from really alone.

And we all three loved that.

PART SIX

MY REAL FAMILY

Chapter Twenty-Six

D o ghosts dream? Not a normal question in normal conversation.

It never dawned on me that when I died I would keep dreaming.

In fact, until I died I didn't know ghosts slept. Hadn't given it one ounce of thought, to be honest. But we do. We sleep, eat, go to the bathroom, get sweaty, and can get rip-roaring drunk on some occasions.

We also can have great sex and help live humans with all sorts of problems from self-confidence to stopping smoking to losing weight to preventing suicide and murder.

On top of all that, we dream. But in the first months of being dead, that wasn't something I noticed.

Until three nights ago when I started dreaming about Topaz.

My parents were a weird couple by any definition and they decided, for some reason lost with their deaths, that they should name their daughters after stones. I was the oldest and they called me Marble. Their second child, two years younger than me, was named Diamond. And our baby sister, ten years younger than me, was named Topaz.

Now I was born in 1910. And during my earlier years as a superhero I had to fake my death so that my not getting older wouldn't be very clear to my aging parents and Diamond.

Topaz, on the other hand, we lost when she was just four. One moment she was there playing on the stoop in front of our home, the next she had just vanished. The police thought she was kidnapped, but there was never a ransom note.

It almost destroyed my parents and Diamond and I had to step up and help with everything until I finally left the house to marry husband number one, a guy I seldom think about and never talk about. Not only was he a controlling jerk, but he lasted less than thirty seconds when we had sex.

I had wanted to ask him what the point was. Never did.

That marriage ended when he thought he could hit me. He tried once and I left him in a puddle of his own blood on our kitchen floor and never went back.

By the time of my first husband and my developing superhero powers, Topaz vanishing was just a wound I didn't want to open.

So now, over a hundred years later, why I would be dreaming about Topaz made no sense.

None.

But I was.

And I wasn't dreaming about Topaz at four years old. I was dreaming she was my age.

And she was calling to me.

Drove me nuts.

Twice I woke up almost sobbing from the dream and poor Sims had to hold me against her to get me to calm down enough to tell her the dream.

Finally, after I had the dream three nights in a row, Sims was waiting for me in the kitchen when I came out of the shower. Our real-life superhero roommate, Canyon, was off at work.

"So what are we going to do about the dreams?" Sims asked. "From the looks of your eyes, I assume you had another one this morning after I got up."

I just nodded and sipped on my coffee. Outside our condo windows, the sun had the city of Las Vegas in bright contrast and it already looked like it would be a warm day.

Our condo was modern and bright and had one of the best views in the entire city, but not even the view right now was helping me.

Sims and I took our coffee and went out to the table on the patio outside. A slight breeze kept the air just cool enough to make it nice and it relaxed me.

"Not sure what we can do about the dreams," I said after we got settled.

"We search for Topaz," Sims said. "She is calling to you for a reason."

"You do remember she vanished over a hundred years ago?"

Sims smiled. "Doesn't mean she still isn't around in some fashion or another."

She pointed at me and then at herself.

I laughed and nodded to her point.

Sims was actually a few years older than I was, but after a hundred years we had jokingly decided that a few years shouldn't make any difference in our relationship.

"So how do we search for my missing sister?" I asked.

Sims only shrugged. "I don't know, but we got to try."

And with that, I agreed.

CHAPTER TWENTY-SEVEN

We decided to ask our friend and immediate boss in the ghost world, Jewel, if she could help us.

A moment after I called to her, she appeared.

Jewel, like Sims and I, dressed casually every day. Today all three of us had on jeans, tennis shoes, and expensive blouses. My blouse was blue, Sims had on a pink one, Jewel's blouse was tan. All of us had our long hair pulled back off our faces. Today I had gone to an off-pink color.

I believed in being comfortable most of the time when alive. Now that I was dead and very few people could see me, comfort was an everyday thing for me. Although I did like to look good for Sims and I did like messing with the color of my hair. A girl or ghost has to have hobbies after all.

Jewel grabbed a chair on the patio and sat down.

"This doesn't look like an emergency," she said, smiling and indicating the fantastic view and our two cups of coffee.

"Not a run-like-hell emergency," I said. "But an urgent problem we're trying to figure out."

I then told her about dreaming about my sister and how she had vanished over a hundred years before, yet was now calling me for help as an adult about my age.

"Could she be a superhero or a Ghost Agent?" Sims asked.

Jewel nodded. "Sounds like she might be. And it has been known to have superheroes exist out of the same family. Something about the genes I have yet to figure out and keep forgetting to ask someone who might know."

I liked the sounds of superheroes running in families. I had never known Topaz, really, since she was so young when she was taken. But it would be nice to have a sister if we could find her now.

"Anyone we can ask?" Sims asked.

Jewel shook her head. "Maybe Laverne would know."

The idea of bothering Lady Luck herself with my dreams just made me shudder.

We sat there in silence, the slight breeze blowing across us, the sounds of the downtown area of Las Vegas filling the air from below.

Finally Jewel said, "Any hints as to where she is at from your dreams?"

I sat back at that, surprised at not thinking of that myself.

I nodded after a moment, trying to bring the dream back

up out here in the bright light. It felt fuzzy and I couldn't get a hold on it completely. All I could really feel was the emotion of sadness and wanting me.

I glanced at Sims, then at Jewel. "Would one of you mind going into my mind and seeing if you can watch the dream for details?"

Sims pointed to Jewel.

Jewel shrugged. "I can try."

She stood and moved over and sat down on me, like she was sitting on my lap.

Only she vanished.

I didn't feel a thing.

"It doesn't echo in here," Jewel said.

Her voice was as clear inside my head as if she was sitting beside me.

I laughed. "Not funny."

"Okay, I'm at the dream," Jewel said. "Repeat this to Sims as I report it. Topaz is a woman about your age. Looks like you, actually."

"Topaz is my age and looks like me in my dream," I said to Sims.

"She is in a hotel room with the blinds open, about twenty floors up, and I can see the Bellagio Hotel tower through the window in the distance."

I was starting to get excited.

"She's here in Vegas in a hotel room," I said to Sims who brightened up with that news.

"She is not trapped or being held prisoner," Jewel said. "And she is very much alive. She is just waiting."

Jewel stood and moved back over to her chair.

"I didn't feel a thing," I said. "Just heard your voice."

Jewel smiled. "Good."

"So can we find her?" Sims asked a moment before I could.

"From the view out her window," Jewel said, "she appears to be in the MGM main tower."

"We can search the rooms," Sims said.

"I didn't get a sense she was calling out to you in the dreams," Jewel said. "She was mourning you. That's what you were feeling."

It never occurred to me that I would be mourned in any fashion, let alone by a sister I had figured had been dead for a hundred years.

Sims stood and offered her hand to me. "Let's go find her and find out exactly what she is doing here."

I nodded and took my partner's hand and a moment later Jewel jumped us to the hallway on the twentieth floor of the MGM Grand hotel.

And we found my long-dead, but now very-much-alive sister just ten minutes later.

Chapter Twenty-Eight

"Wow, she does look like you," Sims said as all three of us stood just inside Topaz's room.

Topaz had dark brown hair, my natural color when I didn't dye it blue or purple or some other rainbow color. She had the same shaped face and eyes and everything.

And she was even dressed the same way the rest of us were, in jeans, tennis shoes, and a nice blouse.

She was sitting at a round table in front of her window, looking out over the Strip toward the Bellagio in the distance.

It was like I had actually walked into my own dream.

Creepy, just creepy.

Part of me wanted this woman to be Topaz, part of me didn't believe it was possible.

"You want to see why she is here?" Sims asked me.

I just shook my head. I wasn't sure I wanted to know. And honestly, I was worried if I was about to wake up sobbing again and all this was just another dream.

"I can do it," Jewel said and started toward Topaz, or whoever she was. At that moment there was a knock at the door.

Jewel stopped and the three of us moved out of the way against the wall as Topaz went to the door and opened it.

"Thanks for seeing me," Topaz said, stepping back and allowing her guest to come in.

"My pleasure," Patty Ledgerwood said, stepping into the room. "Always glad to help."

Having my good friend Patty show up was about as shocking as anything so far. What in the world was going on?

Patty took two steps into the room and froze as she saw the three of us standing there like ghost statues against the wall.

I just shrugged and smiled.

Sims made a motion to say nothing.

Jewel just laughed and waved and shook her head.

"Can I get you a bottle of water," Topaz said.

I was surprised. Topaz's voice sounded a lot like mine as well.

"I'm fine," Patty said, going over to the table and sitting where Topaz had indicated. From there she could see us clearly.

"So tell me, what kind of information do you need?"

"I was in Boise a few weeks back and happened to run

across a picture of two murder victims," Topaz said. "The woman was listed as Marble Grant, my sister's name, and she looked just like me."

"And you are wondering if Marble Grant was a superhero, since the only way she might be alive that long is to be one?"

"That, yes," Topaz said, nodding. "Or if there is someone special among the superheroes and gods who could help me trace exactly what happened to my real family. This woman might have been a granddaughter of my sister or something."

Patty looked puzzled. "Weren't you in contact with your family?"

Topaz shook her head. "Turns out I was kidnapped by another family when I was four and only learned the truth when my mother was on her deathbed. My kidnapping mother. By that point all of my real family was dead or had vanished. Until I saw that picture, I didn't think to even wonder about family, to be honest."

Patty nodded, then looked over at me.

It was clear, she was waiting for me to make a decision.

"You need to tell her," Sims said, holding my hand and squeezing it.

I nodded. "Get Topaz ready for what is about to happen. And can you help her see us?"

"I can't, but Laverne can," Patty said.

"What?" Topaz asked, clearly confused at what Patty had just said out of the blue.

Patty smiled and turned slightly to face Topaz. "You have

been living in Madison, right? As a superhero of accounting and numbers and computing."

Topaz nodded.

Wow, I was stunned. My baby sister was a math whiz.

"I have a story to tell you," Patty said, smiling. "You know I have been around a very long time?"

"You and Poker Boy and your team have saved the world a few times," Topaz said. "That's why I came to you for help."

"For most of the last one hundred years, two of my closest friends were two women named Sims and Marble. Both superheroes."

With that Topaz actually jerked and sat up like she might spring from the chair at any moment.

"That was Marble you saw in the photo. Your sister. In fact you two look almost identical."

"Oh, no," Topaz said shrinking down into the chair like a deflated balloon. "She's dead. I missed her."

I just shook my head and Sims hugged me for comfort.

"I lost my other good friend Sims a few months later," Patty said.

"I am so sorry," Topaz said.

"Have you ever heard of Ghost Agents?" Patty asked.

"I heard rumors that ghosts working with superheroes helped save the world last Christmas. I thought it was just silliness."

Sims and Jewel and I laughed. My poor baby sister was going to be in for a massive shock very shortly.

"No, Ghost Agents are very real," Patty said. "They are

selected for their skills to not move on into the next life, but stick around as ghosts to help others."

Topaz now looked puzzled, which I am sure would be like if I had stared in the mirror with a puzzled look. Amazing how much we looked alike.

"Laverne," Patty said. "A little help if you wouldn't mind."

Patty nodded and then said, "Thank you."

Topaz was sitting so she wasn't looking directly at us.

"Why are you asking Lady Luck for..."

Then she saw us and almost went over backward in her chair, catching herself at the last minute.

"Good to see you, little sister," I said, smiling so hard I felt like my face might just explode and make a ghost mess everywhere.

Topaz looked at me, then at Sims, then at Jewel, then back to Patty. All of us were smiling.

"This isn't a joke?"

"No joke," Patty said. "Marble, Sims, and Jewel there are all three Ghost Agents. Laverne allowed you to see them is all."

Topaz just stared at me for a moment.

And then, without warning, she broke into sobs and came toward me to hug me.

And by the time I got to her I was crying as well.

Sims and Patty and Jewel were also crying.

Five women in a hotel room crying in happiness.

It was a horrid mess.

Thankfully, not a one of us wore makeup.

PART SEVEN

A GIRL'S GOT TO DRINK

CHAPTER TWENTY-NINE

W ho knew ghosts could get drunk?
    But I was a ghost and most definitely drunk. Tipsy as someone might say.

Sloshed.

Feeling no pain.

And Sims, my beautiful blonde, very hot partner, also seemed to be under the influence of the ten or so Gray Goose vodka sliders we had managed to put down. Her wonderful, intense blue eyes didn't seem to be able to focus.

I know I was focused on her. I wanted to get us both back to our apartment, get us both out of these slinky dresses we had poured ourselves into earlier, and see what kind of trouble we could get into on our huge soft bed.

At least before one of us got sick and had to hold the

other's hair over the toilet. Got a hunch that was coming as well unless us ghosts had a way of suddenly getting sober.

Damn wouldn't that be nice.

We were in our newest favorite bar just off the Strip.

Music was loud, the dancing fast, the drinks real, and everyone in the place was young. The lighting moved from a strobe to the beat to dark and moody. Somewhere under all the bodies I figured there was dark wood furniture, a wooden floor, and enough spilled liquor to glue a house together without nails.

At first we had taken turns being inside hot young couples, dancing, enjoying how all they wanted was to get laid. It was infectious, I can say that much. Young hormones were powerful things.

And after we had five or six drinks, we just started dancing on our own, not caring how many people went through us because everyone was thinking the same thing we were thinking about getting laid. We were in love with each other and this was our night out, date night, so we didn't care.

But wow was I horny.

And drunk. Don't forget the drunk part.

About the eighth drink, we found a table and sat. The couple at the table hadn't returned in thirty minutes and from the looks of them on the dance floor, they wouldn't return to do anything but get their things and head for a room. Just watching their young bodies pressing together made me hot.

One thing both Sims and I had discovered early about

being ghosts was that the ghost element of everything tasted so much better than the real thing. Food tasted better, sex felt better, and clearly alcohol was more powerful in ghost form as well.

We started on the Gray Goose vodka shooters because two very rich couples at a table in a VIP area were drinking them. We just took the ghost versions of their drinks. The nice thing about being a ghost was the real people never noticed.

But wow did we notice.

Those drinks tasted wonderful and clearly had a kick.

"Is the room spinning?" Sims asked as the sound dimmed slightly. She smiled at me across the table, but her smile was a little sideways.

Oh, oh. We needed to get moving before ghost puke ended up all over everything.

"That's just me wanting to get you home in bed and do wonderful things to that body of yours," I said, standing and offering her my hand, surprised I had managed a full sentence in my drunken state.

"We can't drive," she said. "We're too drunk."

Then she giggled.

Damn I loved her giggle.

I was just about to jump us to our wonderful bed when the couple returned to their table and he went right through me.

Suddenly my delightfully dizzy feeling was gone, replaced by total horror.

This guy was planning on killing his date tonight after

they finished. That way his wife would never know he had cheated on her.

He had done the same to some poor girl a year ago at this same real estate conference he was attending.

The guy's name was Radford. He sold real estate back in the Midwest and was here only for the conference. He was cold and calculating and I'll tell you, his mind could kill a girl's buzz faster than dropping a cell phone in a toilet.

I pulled Sims toward me and she went through him as well. I needed my partner on the same page with me on this one. Two drunk ghosts might be equal to one sober one.

I hoped.

Sims shivered and looked at the guy like a mother about to scold a child.

"Now that's not right," she said, staring at the monster. "You can have sex with someone without killing them, you pervert."

I laughed and hugged my partner around the shoulders.

"You take the girl," I said. "Make her so dizzy she's got to sit down and then throw up."

Sims laughed and gave me a drunken thumbs-up. "Now that should be easy and I might just join her. Damn room is spinning like someone jacked up the speed on a merry-go-round."

She went into the woman who instantly sat down where I had been sitting. The poor woman went from flushed-pink horny to a strange shade of green almost instantly.

Sims appeared, shaking her beautiful head and frowning. A drunken frown, but still a frown.

"She was planning on killing him tonight so her husband wouldn't find out." Sims stared at both of them. "He's evil and she's an ice queen. What a pair. They deserve each other."

"What the hell?" I asked.

"A real winner," Sims said. "Take a look but don't over-stay your welcome. She's about to blow."

I went over and went inside the woman who was clearly about to be sick. Sims was right. Last year she had killed a guy she slept with to make sure her powerful husband back east wouldn't find out what she had done here while on a trip with the girls.

I stepped back out of the ice queen to join Sims just as the woman lost part of her drinks all over her expensive slutty black shoes and his expensive silk suit pants.

"Get him to toss his cookies in her hair," Sims said, laughing.

I jumped inside of the monster and figured out quickly how to make him very dizzy and sick to his stomach and then positioned him in such a way that he was standing over her, like he was trying to help her.

Then I got the hell out before how he was feeling made me sick as well.

He threw up some really disgusting blue and black stuff all over his future victim's hair and down inside the back of her low-cut dress.

Oh, yuck, that had to feel damn awful.

Standing back out of the splatter zone, Sims applauded like she was watching a kids' soccer game.

The real people at neighboring tables were moving as well, most laughing.

When he did that, she sat bolt upright, a look of pure evil in her eyes, then the look in her eyes blurred and got confused and she returned fire, spraying his suit jacket and crotch with some really vile red and pink remains of a drink she more than likely regretted drinking.

That caused the evil bastard to jump back and then return fire as well, hitting the front of her dress and legs this time.

She tried to stand in disgust, slipped on the slime-covered surface and went down into the mess.

He then threw up on her again.

Now over the years I had enjoyed myself a lot in bars, but never had I laughed this hard before.

Sims was bent over double, laughing as well.

And all the live people had formed a circle around the couple, out of splatter range of course, and were laughing.

And holding their noses.

The smell was something awful.

Both of the evil humans were dripping vomit. Their planned night of sex and murder was finished, of that I had no doubt.

He managed to take a deep breath of the foul-smelling air and not throw up again.

Then, with a shudder, he turned and with the crowd

opening a path for him, headed for the front door, leaving his future victim on the floor crying.

If she wasn't such a cold-blooded killer, I would have felt bad for her.

Not a chance.

"Remember their hotel and room numbers?" I asked Sims, who grinned once again when the woman lost even more of the pink drink on a poor bouncer's shoes.

"I sure do," she said. "You thinking we deal with them early in the morning?"

"I am," I said.

She reached out and took my hand, giving me that seductive smile I loved so much. "Take me home and do rude things to me."

I took us to our bathroom in our wonderful condo and then standing under a wonderful warm shower, we undressed each other, peeling slowly out of our dresses.

And I don't think that anything we did to each other was rude.

Nope.

However, what we did to the two killers the next morning was rude by any measure, ending with the police hauling both of their hung-over asses to jail for their crimes from the previous year. For some reason they both felt they had to confess over and over.

But that night, after we got home from the bar, still feeling the drinks, every wonderfully dizzy moment with the love of my ghost life was magnificent. I would talk about it, but a good girl doesn't have sex with another good girl and tell.

That wouldn't be proper.

And trust me we were both damn good.

But I do have to admit, what Sims did with her tongue for about thirty minutes was far from proper. Not rude, but not proper either.

I'm dead and I called it heavenly.

CHAPTER THIRTY

A couple nights later, from where I stood off to one side of the Fremont Street Experience, leaning against the stone wall of the Golden Nugget Casino, I could watch a woman with long blonde hair, a tight white blouse, jeans, and expensive tennis shoes.

She was hot, not temperature hot, since the night was a comfortable seventy degrees. I mean drop-dead sexy hot. Long brown hair, huge brown eyes, and a smile that could give a dead man an erection.

And she looked drunk.

Staggering drunk, in a sexy, hot way. Kind of like I hoped I had looked to Sims a few nights before.

Around me and Sims, the craziness of downtown Las Vegas swirled like a midway at a carnival. An X-rated carnival with a twist of New Orleans French Quarter tossed in. There were men wearing g-strings who shouldn't ever wear g-strings, women with basically nothing on willing to pose with anyone for a few bucks right beside every cartoon character imaginable.

I was pretty sure that in the books Sleeping Beauty didn't have to compete with Amazon-sized woman beside her wearing armor from the waist down.

Three bands played along the street about a block or so apart with crowds dancing in front of the stages. And everyone carried a drink.

The entire four-block-long street party was covered by a ninety-foot-high dome of lights. Making it impossible to walk a straight line down the big mall were more small booths and bars than should be crammed into four blocks of space.

Overhead people screamed as they went flying by on a zip-line, just under the dome roof. And the half-dozen major casinos that fronted the Experience all had their doors wide open like hungry mouths welcoming in the food they called tourists.

I honestly loved the Experience, even as tacky and stupid as it was. It had a life to it every night, seven nights a week. And to ghosts like me and Sims, feeling alive was important.

Besides, we only lived about three blocks from the Experience, so wandering through here regularly was something we just did.

"You looking at what I'm looking at?" Sims asked as the hot blonde sort of stumbled into a guy with his wife and daughter in tow. The blonde said something to the poor guy who looked flustered and the guy's wife looked shocked and yanked the guy away.

Sims glanced over at me and smiled. "I think she just propositioned that poor guy."

"I think you might be right," I said, laughing.

"Think she might be interested in two women ghosts?" Sims asked.

"I know I would be interested in finding out what she is thinking," I said, laughing, as we both started across the mall toward her.

When trying to go from one place to another through crowds, we had three choices. We could either walk through people and get glimpses of all of their thoughts and memories, we could try to avoid as many as we could, which meant some tricky side-stepping and ducking moves, or we could just tele-port, or jump as we called it, to the other side.

When working the Experience, Sims and I liked to try to avoid. More fun and some pretty good exercise.

I reached the hot blonde first and faded inside her. A few seconds later Sims joined me.

But I didn't notice exactly when Sims joined me because this woman was the horniest woman I had ever seen. It was like waves and waves of desire cascaded through her mind.

I damn near had an orgasm just trying to get a grip on what I was sensing in this woman's mind.

"Holy shit!" Sims said, breathing hard.

The woman was named Maryalice without a hyphen and

she was in Vegas alone, trying to make herself forget her boyfriend.

"We got to get her off this street," I said to Sims through what felt like an intense red haze inside the woman's mind.

"No kidding," Sims said, seeming to shout even though I could hear her fine. "She's on some sort of drug."

I could feel the woman's heart racing, her breath getting shorter and shorter. She was just about to overdose right here in the middle of this crowd.

"Get her over against the casino wall and I'll get help," I said to Sims.

I stepped out of the woman, shuddering at how the entire sexual feelings still sort of hung around me like moss off a tree. That might take some release to clear later tonight with Sims. Wow.

A handsome young security cop was about fifty feet away. I jumped into him and got him turned and headed through the crowd toward the woman at full run.

He was young and gay and loved the strangeness of the crowds at the Experience as well. His partner worked in one of the nearby casinos and they had a dog named Spot because it had been hard to apartment train.

Sims had gotten the hot blonde over to the wall and had her sitting on the concrete.

Her face looked sickly white and her eyes were closed.

I had the cop call for emergency medical help before he even got to the woman, making him understand the woman was overdosing on something.

Sims hadn't appeared from the woman yet.

So when the cop kneeled down beside the woman who now looked like she was passing out, I went back inside of her.

Sims was doing her best to hold the woman together.

But we both knew almost instantly we were too late. This woman's body was shutting down and shutting down hard.

"We need to get out of here now," I said to Sims. "We don't want to be in here when she dies."

"What would happen if we were?" Sims asked as I joined her to try to keep the woman's heart pumping just a little longer.

"We'll figure that out later," I said.

I knew there were many reasons I loved Sims so much. But one was her fight and the fact she just wasn't willing to let go against all odds.

But at the last possible second, Sims did and both of us got out of the dying woman's body just as she took her last breath.

CHAPTER THIRTY-ONE

We stepped back and leaned against the wall and out of the way as paramedics arrived and started CPR. A half-circle of gawkers formed around them as they worked.

But Sims and I both knew Maryalice was dead.

Dead far before she had really gotten a chance to do much living.

Damn it. If we had gotten to her sooner we might have been able to save her.

Then a voice beside us said simply, "Well that sucks. All I wanted to do was get laid."

Both Sims and I spun around to face Maryalice's ghost, staring down at her own body being worked over by the paramedics. The cop that I had fetched was watching, his face in shock.

"I wonder if he would be interested in doing it with a dead girl?" Maryalice said, moving toward the cop.

"Hang on," I said.

The woman turned and looked at me, then at her body on the ground, then back at me. "You are dead too?"

"We both are," Sims said.

"You two were in my head trying to save me, weren't you?"

I nodded.

"Nice of you."

"What did you take to cause that?" Sims asked, pointing at the body on the ground with the oxygen mask over her face and someone pumping her chest.

"Not a clue," Maryalice said, shrugging, which made her wonderful breasts do wonderful things. "My old boyfriend gave the pills to me at one point to try to calm my inhibitions. Never tried them until tonight. He was such a bastard I should have known they would do something like this to me."

"Or maybe you took too many?" I asked, smiling at her.

Both Sims and I knew that was what had happened. Maryalice had taken one, didn't feel anything, so took three more with a glass of vodka right before heading for the Experience.

"Yeah, might have done that," she said, laughing. "Too late now I suppose."

She glanced around. "You two the only ghosts around these parts? And why am I still here? Aren't I supposed to be riding some magic light off into another world?"

"You are," Sims said, nodding.

I was worried about that, actually. Was this woman going to be another agent?

At that point the medics on the ground put some sort of tube down Maryalice's throat and started pumping out the contents of her stomach. After they did that, they kept up CPR and oxygen.

"Well, that's gross," Maryalice said, staring at what was being done to her body.

"They are still trying to save you," Sims said.

Suddenly I realized why this woman's light hadn't arrived yet. She wasn't completely disconnected from her body yet, which meant she might be able to be saved.

"What's your old boyfriend's name and where does he live exactly?" I asked.

"Why? Think we can go haunt him?"

"No, I want to find out what the pill was you took," I said. "And I need to do it quickly."

She shrugged and gave me the address in Missoula, Montana and what he looked like and his favorite bar if he wasn't home.

Sims nodded to me that she would watch Maryalice and I jumped to Missoula.

Chapter Thirty-Two

The guy was a slob and his place smelled of old food, too much garbage, and sweat socks.

He was on a recliner watching television and drinking a beer.

I went inside him.

I was stunned that actually he was a pretty good guy. His name was Bobby, an engineering student, and had been really in love with Maryalice when she left him because he liked sex a little more than she seemed to.

And I had seen that Maryalice really loved him as well, but didn't want to disappoint him by not being good enough at sex for him.

The two were so uptight about it, they couldn't even talk.

I quickly found the name of the medication she had taken and jumped back to Vegas.

I winked at Sims and then jumped back into the young cop's mind. I quickly made him believe that Maryalice had told him what she had taken and he needed to tell the paramedics at once.

He leaned down and told the paramedics the name of the pill. One of them asked, "Are you sure?"

"She said she took three of them," I made him say.

Then I left him with that clear memory of talking with her and jumped out.

With that information, the paramedics went into even more of a frenzied action.

"Think they might save my sorry ass?" Maryalice said.

"I think you have a damn fine ass," Sims said.

"I do too," I said, smiling at her.

Maryalice laughed and blushed a little. "You know, I don't normally swing toward women, but for you two I might make an exception."

"Now I'm getting hot," Sims said, pretending to fan herself.

"You know," I said to Maryalice, "your boyfriend is a really nice guy and misses you and really isn't worried about your sex life. He just wants you for who you are."

"How do you know that?" Maryalice asked, staring at me.

"Just spent a few seconds inside his head to get the name of the medication he gave you."

"Oh," Maryalice said.

"He finds you as hot as we do. More than likely that's why you thought he wanted sex too much."

Maryalice blushed again. "Actually, I wanted it as much if not more than he did, but was too embarrassed to tell him, like a fool."

"And we know you love him as well," Sims said.

Maryalice looked all misty-eyed. "I do."

"Then tell him that," I said. "And then jump him and ride him like a bucking bronco in a rodeo."

"How about first you climb back into that hot body of yours there," Sims said, "and give this a real fight."

"And tell Bobby you love him when you see him," I said. "Promise me?"

Maryalice nodded. "How do I get back into that mess?"

"Just go over there and sink down into yourself," Sims said. "I'll take you back inside, get you settled."

"Thanks," Maryalice said. "This has been one whacked-out dream. Hope I remember it?"

"You will," Sims said.

Sims pointed to me. "That's Marble, I'm Sims. Name your and Bobby's kids after us when the time comes."

"I'll do that," Maryalice said.

With that Sims took her hand and the two of them went over and sunk down into Maryalice's body.

A moment later the paramedic shouted, "I got a pulse! Get the stretcher ready for transport."

I was cheering along with the crowd watching.

A few moments later the love of my life appeared and came toward me smiling.

"She's going to be fine," Sims said. "But I'm not."

"What's wrong?" I asked.

Sims smiled. "I'm so damn horny I could jump you right here."

She kissed me hard and I kissed her back and after a wonderful, long minute, we came up for air.

"Think anyone would notice us?" I asked.

"That might be half the fun," she said, working to get off my blouse at the same time I worked at hers. "We could put out a tip jar."

"We could be rich," I said.

Sims laughed as we slumped to the ground, frantically working on each other's clothes.

Over fifty people walked right through us over the next forty minutes as Sims and I let off some massive pent-up steam, so to speak.

Some of the people who walked through us would have been appalled.

But most would have just thought it another Fremont Street Experience.

That's why I loved this place so much.

Almost anything goes. After all, it is Vegas.

PART EIGHT

ONE-YEAR ANNIVERSARY

Chapter Thirty-Three

How does a person go about celebrating the one-year anniversary of being dead?

I honestly have no idea. Not something you get a Hallmark card for.

I'm not sure I should be celebrating maybe one of the stupidest deaths on record. If I had had to take the tunnel to the white light and not stay over and be a Ghost Agent and meet Sims, I would have been annoyed at myself for eternity. How can a superhero who can instantly teleport to a different location get shot in the head by a drug addict?

Well, I managed it.

So now it was coming up on the one-year anniversary of my death and my wonderful partner and lover, Sims, had asked me what I wanted to do to celebrate. Besides spending the night in bed making love to her, which is always my first answer to most questions, I had no idea.

She said we had a few days to decide and I agreed. I was leaning toward drinking, dancing, and massive amounts of sex when we ran across a guy wandering around a local grocery store looking lost and very much down on his luck.

Since Brad was a handsome guy, nearing thirty, who looked like he at least showered at times, Sims said she would take a look in his mind to see what was going on while I glimpsed into the mind of an unhappy and, as I discovered, unfaithful housewife who had been staring at the boxes of corn flakes like they might explode if she touched one.

Seems the housewife fed her two young children corn flakes every morning and was feeling so guilty about the romp in the hay the previous night, she wasn't sure about her ability to still be a good mother.

From what I could tell, the sex had been full of guilt for both parties and there had been tears, never a good thing after sex.

I quickly eased back the guilt, gave her the resolve to not do it again until the kids were out of school, and never ever tell her poor husband that she loved beyond measure.

If it had been great sex, I might have left that part out, but the sex was in the dark, with half their clothes still on, and far, far too quick. Husband didn't need to know about that. It almost didn't actually count as sex.

When I left her mind she sort of nodded to herself and

put two boxes of corn flakes in the cart. I think I just saved her two kids years of therapy.

"Marble," Sims said. "You are not going to believe this?"

She pointed to the handsome and clearly lost guy who still seemed to be trying to make up his mind between a box of macaroni and cheese and a tuna helper.

"Let me guess," I said. "He's broke."

"Not really," Sims said. "He's trying to conserve his money because he wants more time to keep looking for his parents."

"His parents?"

Sims nodded and I could see the concern in her eyes that she really cared about this guy's problem.

"His parents just vanished. No trace," Sims said. "Take a look."

I nodded and we both went into the guy's mind.

His name was Brad Young, fairly smart, very driven, and Jim and Jean Young's youngest child.

The entire story was sort of laid out in Brad's mind like a movie since he was so, so intently focused on it.

Kansas City natives Jim and Jean Young loved the feel of Las Vegas in the winter more than anywhere in the world. They often brought their twenty-two-foot RV to a small trailer park thirty miles west of the city and stayed for three months, from right after Christmas to late March, to escape the Midwest winters.

"Can't blame them for that," I said.

Sims said, "Got that right."

The movie of Brad's problem just went scrolling on and I could see that the intensity and repetition of it was slowly driving Brad crazy. Sleeping for him was only optional at times.

It seemed that both of Brad's parents had worked hard most of their lives to have this kind of freedom. Their kids and grandkids loved the fact that Grandma and Grandpa got out of town on their own every year.

Grandpa Jim, at five-five and almost round, had diabetic foot pain and didn't much like all the walking. So they always took a shuttle from their trailer park into the Strip and spent one day exploring just one hotel.

Just one. They took their time, sitting a lot, enjoying the feel and excitement of the place, even though neither of them liked to gamble at all.

It took them all winter to see every major hotel and casino in Vegas at three hotels a week. They loved the challenge and had a map of all the major casinos that they would spread on the table in their motor home and mark off each hotel.

"That is dedication to a hobby," I said.

"I find it sweet," Sims said.

I wanted to hug the love of my life, but since we were in Brad's mind, that was tough to do.

Jim and Jean also loved to collect the casino player's cards and had notebooks full of them after doing the Vegas trip for five winters.

But most of all they loved the food. Like Jim, Jean wasn't

a small woman. She towered over Jim and outweighed him and had long since gone to what she called "square" in shape.

Brad loved how his parents considered themselves expert eaters, usually hitting the casino buffet for lunch and then the casino steak house for dinner on each trip into the Strip.

Eating through the winter was actually the focus of their lives. And they loved it.

I had to admit, eating was a focus of my life as well, but because I am a ghost agent and dead, the food tasted even better. Plus Sims and I exercised enough to keep our weights under control. Who knew ghosts could gain weight.

Jean kept meticulous notes of every meal and what they thought about it and what it cost them. And then the next year they made sure to avoid the bad restaurants and return to the good ones.

For the last five years they had used Facebook to let their family in on their restaurant finds on a daily basis and had a large following of over two hundred family and friends who lived through Jean's glowing, or not-so-glowing, reports of the day's adventures.

When it got to late March, their stay for the winter was almost over. And both of them were looking forward to getting back to their routines and their grandkids in Kansas.

This was when Brad's mind started getting angry and confused and his story became a jumble. From what I could tell, with one week left before leaving, something happened that made no sense to anyone.

Jim and Jean Young simply vanished.

They had last been seen getting on the shuttle from the RV park. The small bus was driven by a man by the name of Harry Krist. The shuttle was never found.

No sign at all of Jim, Jean, or Harry could be found. And no sign of violence in the slightest.

To the Las Vegas police, the very strange missing person's case never got off the ground.

But Brad Young, Jim and Jean's youngest child, didn't think the case should be left to the police. So he took a leave from his high-paying tech job and moved into his parents' small trailer outside of Vegas and spent every day trying to retrace their movements and figure out what had happened.

He was having no luck.

None at all. And it had been six days now.

To Brad six long, impossible days.

CHAPTER THIRTY-FOUR

Sims planted some calming thoughts in Brad's mind and the idea that sleep and regular eating would help him think clearer, then the two of us stepped back into the noise of the supermarket. Brad shook his head at the tuna helper section and headed for the meat section. At least we had helped him eat better.

"So, think we can help him find his parents?" Sims asked.

I just laughed and said, "I think we can try. But neither one of us have proven to be great detectives."

"But we know one," Sims said, smiling.

I also was smiling at the many wonderful nights we had spent in our big bed with the world's best woman detective, Sky Tate.

Sky was a live superhero in the world of detectives and she

was very, very good at what she did not only in bed, but as a detective.

"Let's go see if she has the time to help us," I said.

Sims smiled and kissed me and a moment later we jumped outside the heavy wooden door with thick opaque glass to Sky's office.

"Knock, knock." Sims said in a way that her voice would carry into the office. "Anyone home?"

"What the hell?" Sky said. "You two never need to knock."

A moment later Sims and I were standing in front of Sky's big wooden desk, at the moment covered with a bunch of paperwork.

Sky was smiling with a grin that might split her face as she stood and came around the desk. And she had a wonderful face, with deep dark eyes and a Roman nose that Sky called her "beak." Trust me, that beak could do some wonderful things to a ghost in some very wonderful places.

Sky's normal gray trench coat and hat were on a coat tree stand near the door and Sky had on jeans and a white silk blouse. Almost identical to what Sims and I were wearing.

Sky's office on the second floor of a Strip office was one of those comfortable places with big leather couch and an over-stuffed chair and a fantastic view of the Strip looking north toward the downtown area.

"Sorry to interrupt," I said as Sky indicated we should take the couch and she would sit on the chair.

"Insurance claims for a case I just finished," she said,

waving her hand in disgust at the paperwork. "I buy myself a new Cadillac every year just from the money I get from working an insurance claim or two. Sort of a game to keep myself amused between challenging cases."

Then she looked at me and then at Sims. "Why do I have a hunch this might be a fun case that brought you both here?"

"Don't know how fun," Sims said. "But we ran into a Brad Young a little bit ago."

"The guy from back east looking for his missing parents?" Sky asked.

I was surprised. "You working the case?"

"Oh, no," she said, shaking her head. "His story has just been all over the newspapers. Guess ghosts don't read papers, huh?"

I just laughed and shook my head. It had never occurred to me to be honest.

"So we thought we would see what we could find out," Sims said. "You up for helping?"

Again that wonderful smile of Sky's split her face and her eyes lit up and she clapped her hands. "Oh, hell, yes."

Sims and I both laughed.

"So which one of you is going to feed me his story you got from his mind?"

We both stood at the same time, grinning at Sky.

"I think we both should, don't you, Sims?"

"Oh, absolutely," Sims said.

"Now girls," Sky said, laughing as I stepped toward her. "We're on a case here."

"Ain't that going to be a fun case," I said as I sunk inside her and Sims followed me.

A moment later Sky just sat back in her chair and moaned. You can't have two horny ghosts crawling around inside your mind and not moan. But it was a good moan.

Let me just say it took a little while for me and Sims to get Sky the entire story from Brad Young's mind.

A very pleasurable little while.

CHAPTER THIRTY-FIVE

After Sky recovered from her gathering information voyage, she went into her office restroom, splashed some water on her face, combed her long brown hair and put it back up on the top of her head, then came out and sat on the edge of her desk.

"How about I talk to the lead detective on this case," Sky said. "A guy by the name of Danny Lawrence."

"Superhero?" I asked.

"Unfortunately no," Sky said. "But a good guy."

"No need for one of us to crawl around in his head, see what he is hiding?" I asked.

"Nope," Sky said. "Danny is as straight a shooter as they come."

I shrugged and so did Sims. Talking to him was better than any idea we had, which was none.

Sims called the detective that she clearly had on speed dial.

"Danny," she said.

He said something and she laughed. "Actually serious. Need some information on the missing person case with those two senior citizens and a bus driver."

She nodded, then said, "Not working for him directly," she said, "but might be shortly."

I knew that he had asked if she was working for Brad Young. A logical question.

At that point she clicked it over to speakerphone.

"Not a whole hell of a lot I can tell you," Detective Lawrence said. "I wish there was. This stupid case is one of those that's giving me sleepless nights. Those three were seen leaving the Sundowner trailer park that is up off of 95 at eight a.m. sharp. The bus went past two traffic cams on the way into town. All three occupants in the bus looked fine on both of those images."

"I'm assuming the bus never made it to the third traffic cam," Sky said.

"Bingo," the detective said. "That camera is at the intersection up to Sky Canyon and up Mt Charleston. So they never went up that way and there are almost no turn-offs between the second traffic cam and that intersection. We checked them all."

"They had to go somewhere," Sky said.

"That they did and as soon as I figure out where, we can solve this monster."

"Anything twisted or out of place with the bus driver?" Sky asked.

"Nothing. Sixty-six, married, retired from a casino downtown, likes getting out and driving people his age around. His disappearance is as strange as the Youngs'. I think his wife and three kids are going to go crazy real quick if we don't solve this."

"Brad Young is already on the way there from what I understand."

"Yeah, sadly so," Detective Lawrence said.

"And that's it?" Sky asked, looking at me and Sims for any other ideas to ask him. We both just shook our heads.

"That's it," Detective Lawrence said. "And if you do get anything more, please let me know. Hate to retire from the force next year with this still hanging out there. And after six days now I'm losing hope that they might be still alive."

"You got it," Sky said. "I'll see what I can do. Thanks!"

"Glad to know you're looking into this as well," Detective Lawrence said and hung up.

"Well," Sky said. "This is making no sense at all."

All I could do was agree with her.

No sense, no method, no motive. Strange things happened in Vegas, but not like this.

Chapter Thirty-Six

Sky just shook her head and then stood from where she had been half-leaning, half-sitting on the corner of her large wood desk.

"How about I go get us all some burgers and fries for lunch," she said. "If you two wouldn't mind jumping out to that trailer park and getting a feel of the place. Maybe check out a few residents who are home, see if they sense or know anything."

I glanced at Sims and she nodded.

"Cheeseburger, fries, Diet Coke?" Sky said. "That's what I'm having."

"Sounds perfect," I said and Sims again nodded.

"See you in thirty or so," she said and vanished.

I reached out and took Sims' hand and jumped the two of us to the Sundowner Trailer Park.

It was actually nicer and more desolate at the same time than I had gotten the impression of from Brad's mind.

It was tree-lined with both older poplar and palm trees, keeping the entire place shaded. There were paved streets and sidewalks and a large pool complex in the center that looked clean and well-maintained.

It sat right on the highway at a crossroads with a large stone wall separating it from the traffic and the noise. From the looks of it, across the highway there was a large shopping center going in and a housing development behind and beyond it stretching up the slight hill.

"Looks like the Sundowner is about to get swallowed by the growth of the city," I said.

Sims nodded. "Too bad, it's kind of nice."

I agreed. It was, in an old-fashioned 1960s kind of way.

We went along the road to the office and found the manager. An older guy about sixty with no hair and wearing a large hat to keep his bald head from getting too much sun.

The moment we went inside him, I could tell how broken up and scared and worried he was about the three missing people. He felt personally responsible for what happened to them, even though he had no idea what had actually happened.

He was a good man whose wife had died from cancer about ten years before and the Sundowner was all he had. He had inherited the place from his father and loved it.

But now he worried that he wouldn't be able to hold onto it.

He had had lots of offers to sell over the years, but never felt a need to. Now he wasn't so sure. Because of the missing driver and the Youngs, a number of his regulars had moved out and he had a hunch he was going to lose more.

They were all as scared as he was and he didn't blame them.

Sims and I spent the next thirty minutes drifting in and out of anyone we came across. All of them were the same. They had no idea what might have happened, but were scared, worried, and thinking of moving.

It had taken us just over forty minutes when I jumped us back to Sky's office to be greeted by the wonderful smell of hamburger and fries sitting on Sky's desk.

Sims and I both took a ghost hamburger from Sky's plate and used napkins for plates and some fries and took them over to the couch. Nice thing about ghost food is that it doesn't stain.

"You two are sure a cheap date," Sky said, watching us take the ghost portions of her hamburger.

"Oh, the rest of me is where the costs come in," Sims said, giving Sky a sexy smile and a wink.

Sky just fanned herself, pretending to be hot.

I know that smile of Sims made me hot on most days.

"So what kind of mess is the place?" Sky asked before taking a huge bite of hamburger.

Since Sims had just taken a bite as well, I answered.

"Actually a really nice little place, lots of trees, nice pool, well-maintained and newer travel trailers. And it's run by an older guy who really cares about the place."

"Been in his family for a lot of years," Sims said around her mouthful of burger.

"He had nothing at all to do with the disappearance and neither did any of the others we ran into," I said. "They were mostly just all scared."

Sky nodded. "That's understandable."

I took a bite of the fantastic hamburger and we all just sort of sat there eating and thinking.

CHAPTER THIRTY-SEVEN

After we finished the hamburger, Sky tossed the wrappers into the trash beside her desk and sat back. We were all still sipping on our Diet Cokes, and I noticed that even though we were on the Strip, not a sound seemed to get into this office.

"It seems the reason we are so stumped has two sides to it?" Sky said. "Two major questions. First off, we don't know how they vanished."

"Or where they are now," I said.

Sky nodded. "We figure out the answer to the how question, I bet the answer to that will be evident. Or at least I hope it will."

"So what's the second question?" Sims asked.

"Why?" Sky said. "There has to be a how and a why to all crimes."

"That a detective rule?" I asked.

"Human nature rule," Sky said, smiling.

"Logical," Sims said.

"So can you get from your detective friend the traffic camera film of that bus going by before it vanished?" I asked. "Maybe we can see something they missed."

"Worth a try," Sky said.

She took out her cell phone and a few moments later she got permission to take a look at the recordings, but we would have to do it there.

"Thanks," she said to the detective. "See you in thirty."

"Okay," she said, "we see if we can tackle the how."

"I also think that later," I said, "we do some deep diving into the past of the Youngs and the driver, see if there is something in their backgrounds that would lead us to the why."

"I got a superhero friend named Barbara who is an expert in modern computer work," Sky said. "We exchange favors at times and at the moment she owes me."

"I like the look on your face when you said she owes you," I said.

"Sounds yummy," Sims said, smiling.

Sky laughed. "Not in the way your two dirty minds went to immediately."

I noticed that Sky said nothing more. Just smiled.

Ten minutes later we were piled into Sky's brand new golden Cadillac, headed for the main police station downtown. There was just no safe place for Sky to jump to close to the station, so we actually had to drive. That was a new, and honestly kind of fun feeling. I hadn't been in a car except to sit and talk with someone since I died.

I had forgotten how much I loved to ride in a car. What a strange thing to forget after only a year.

CHAPTER THIRTY-EIGHT

Detective Lawrence was just about the most average older detective I could imagine. Right out of central casting for detectives. His suit was just slightly too large, and he had bushy dark eyebrows and thick white hair that looked almost afraid of a comb.

But his eyes were intense and smart and I had no doubt he had a big heart. I liked him instantly.

And he and Sky clearly had a mutual like and respect thing going on. Clearly they had some history.

"Still drives me crazy how you never age," Lawrence said.

"You haven't aged a year either," Sky said, patting his shoulder. "But make you a deal, let's don't go looking at old photos."

"Deal," Lawrence said, laughing as he finished getting her set up on a computer in a side room off what looked like a large cluster of offices and desks. The place was all very modern and brightly lit. Not at all what I had expected or remembered seeing on dozens of cop shows.

He logged in and brought up the file with the images of the bus going by traffic cams, then stepped back enough.

I pushed in beside Sky and Sims did the same as Sky ran the images of the bus passing the two traffic cams.

I didn't see anything at all, but Sims did.

"Green in the seat behind the driver," Sims said. "Something meant to look like the seat, but not exactly."

"Detective," Sky said. "Take a look at this. Can you freeze it?"

The detective moved in beside Sky and Sims barely got out of the way in time.

The detective's large fingers flew over the keyboard and then the image froze.

It still took a moment for me to see it, then when I did it was obvious. Something disguised to match the seat color was on the seat behind the driver.

"I'll be go to hell," Detective Lawrence said. "Someone's on that seat, ducked down."

"Betting on a gun pointed at the driver," Sky said.

"No bet," the detective said, turning and striding into the other room to what must have been his desk.

He pulled out what looked to me like a map and brought it back into the room and spread it out beside the computer.

I could tell it was a map of the highway between the trailer park and the intersection where the bus was not seen.

"Only three roads that bus could have turned off on," Lawrence said. "All three go up into the rocks and dead-end, one at a construction site, two at turn-arounds."

"Equipment at the construction site?" Sky asked.

Lawrence pointed to the road. "There is."

"How much you want to bet they buried the bus," Sky said.

"No damn bet," Lawrence said, yanking out his cell phone and rushing away.

"I'll meet you up there," Sky said to me and Sims. "Good luck."

With that I jumped us to the construction site at the end of the road, scared to death at what we were going to find.

CHAPTER THIRTY-NINE

There was no one around and the entire construction site looked deserted. The air was hot and a wind was blowing dust among some large machines.

I bet the parking area and the area around some piles of lumber wasn't any larger than a parking lot of a fast food place. I could see where what might be the foundation for a large home was pushed up against some rocks.

There were more piles of lumber covered in tarps to one side of the road in.

"Building a house among some of those large rocks," Sims said. "The view will be nice back out over the shallow valley and the highway and Las Vegas in the distance."

"That it will," I said.

"Now what do we do?" Sims asked, slowly turning and looking at everything around us.

"We look for freshly disturbed ground and hope like hell only the bus is under it."

Why in the hell would anyone do this? If we were right, this still made no sense.

It took us a good five minutes of wandering around the construction site and finally jumping up to the top of some rocks over the site before we spotted an area that had been dug.

It was long and rectangle, like they had built a driveway down into the hole as well.

From on top of the rock, we could see where some of the dirt around the slanted roof of the bus had slipped, leaving the bus shape visible in the dirt from above.

"We jump together," Sims said. "Holding hands."

I was very glad she said that. No way I wanted to jump into a buried bus, more than likely with three dead people in it, especially alone.

I nodded to Sims and a moment later, from the top of the rock and bright sun, we were inside the small bus.

It smelled awful, like we had jumped inside of an outhouse. Thankfully the temperature was fairly cool.

There was a very faint amount of light coming through the dirt over a skylight in the bus. It looked like it had cracked under the weight and a sliver of light and a flow of air was coming through.

With that faint light, we could see the Youngs and the bus driver in their seats, their legs cuffed to the chairs.

A dozen empty bottles of water and a couple soda cans littered the area around them, along with some wrappers from what must have been the driver's lunch and some drinks that the Youngs had taken along.

I moved over to the driver and touched him and was shocked to feel he was still alive.

I was certain that the bus wasn't big enough for the oxygen to last, so the air flowing in through the broken skylight had saved them, along with the bottles of water and tiny bits of food, but I doubted the three of them had much longer. He was unconscious and breathing very shallowly.

"The Youngs are alive!" Sims said.

"We got to get help and get help quick," I said and we jumped out of the smell and back into the bright light.

We both stopped for a moment and took deep breaths trying to clear the smell and the memory of being in that buried bus.

"Let's jump to the intersection of the highway," Sims said, "see if help is coming."

At that moment I could hear the sound of a car speeding up the road and then we could see it.

Actually three patrol cars, lights flashing but no sirens.

"Great timing," I said.

As the first one came around the corner into the construction site, I jumped into the patrolman's head. Young guy, loved his wife, his new kid, and playing D&D. He liked being called Danny by his friends and he was very proud that he was a Metro officer.

I planted the thought in his head that the bus was buried and how he could see it with the indent in the dirt. And that there was a chance that the occupants might somehow still be alive.

Sims clearly had done the same thing to the officer sliding to a halt in his car behind Danny's car.

Both officers sprang from their cars and ran toward the bus, both seeing the indent in the dirt.

"Skylight in the top of the bus," I said in Danny's mind.

Danny grabbed a cut two-by-four from a lumber pile and started banging on the ground.

"Echoing," a third officer said.

"These small buses have skylights," Danny said. Then the two-by-four he had been pounding hit the skylight and made a very different sound.

"Here," he shouted. And a moment later he broke the skylight some and dust dropped through a now bigger crack.

All three of the officers started pushing the dirt back until the skylight and top of the bus was visible, then Danny with a massive hit smashed open the skylight with the board.

Then two of them on their stomachs shined their lights into the bus while the other ran back to his car to call for more help.

"I think they are alive," Danny said and I pushed that idea

even more in his mind. "I can see empty water bottles and food wrappers around them."

"I got a gas-operated fan in my trunk for drying a spill," the second cop said that Sims was directing. "Let me see if I can shove a bunch of fresh air down through that hole."

He turned and sprinted for his car as Sims stepped out of him and I stepped out of Danny.

Danny headed for his car to get rope and something to cut the prisoners free and a medical kit and an oxygen tank. Danny might fit through that skylight, maybe, but the three in the bus were far too big to come out that way. They were going to have to wait until the police dug out that door.

Sims took my hand and we just stood there in the warm sun, both smiling, as the three officers scrambled to save the lives in the bus and even more officers arrived, stirring up even more dust.

Finally, to get out of the dust, we jumped up and sat on the rock above the entire scene and just watched.

It was really something to watch as Danny went down through the skylight, got oxygen on all three in the bus, and six other officers using shovels from their cars started digging out the back door of the bus.

It was amazing how fast six strong men and women could dig. They had the back door open just as the first of three ambulances pulled in.

Right behind the second ambulance Sky pulled in right ahead of Detective Lawrence. As she got out she waved at us and then went with the Detective.

And ten minutes later the officers had all three out of the bus and in ambulances and headed for the hospitals.

All three would live, and I couldn't begin to say how good that felt.

Over the last year since I had died, Sims and I had saved our share of lives, but these three seemed even more special.

CHAPTER FORTY

After everything settled down and we had a moment to be alone with Sky, we invited her up to our place for a party because we saved the three people. She declined because she said the case wasn't over yet.

And I knew she was right.

"Sure, we saved the people," she said, "but still no clue who did this and I'm going to stick close to Detective Lawrence to try to help."

So we agreed to meet for lunch the next day so she could update us.

I hate to admit that Sky had been right on not wanting to party yet. Sims and I were emotionally spent, more than I could remember us being in the year we had been working together.

We took a long shower together, then had a nice sushi

dinner, and now we were just sitting on our patio drinking and talking about who might have done this to those three and why.

The night was just about perfect, not too hot, not chilly, and no wind. Perfect patio weather. We spent a lot of the time on some evenings just sort of thinking and staring out over the city on that patio.

I mentioned to Sims that my way of dying a year ago was a lot better than the way those three almost died.

"Mine too," Sims said. "So fast you don't know what hit you. I don't want to think about sitting in the dark for days dying slowly."

"On that note we need more drinks," I said, shuddering.

And I went and got them.

After an hour Canyon got home from a dinner meeting and joined us and we told him the entire story.

"Wow," he said, shaking his head. "Been reading about that in the paper and you two solved it."

I just shook my head. Seems we really needed to read a paper at times.

"Us and Sky, actually," Sims said.

"But not really solved it," I said. "No idea who would do this or why."

"Money," Canyon said, taking a sip of his vodka tonic. Canyon was a superhero in the world of money and finance so his mind just worked that way.

"Always look to the money," he said. "From the sounds of

it these three people had no enemies, so it has to be money. And those three have none, am I right?"

"Nothing worth doing this for," I said.

"So there is other money involved and these three just got in the way somehow, or were in the wrong spot at the wrong time."

Sims looked at me and I looked at her and we both smiled and I said, "I'll tell Sky and be right back."

I jumped to Sky's side as she and Detective Lawrence were having dinner. I was impressed that she didn't even jump when I appeared standing next to their table like a memory of a bad waitress from the past.

"Sorry to interrupt," I said, "but Canyon thinks it might be money behind this and the owner of the Sundowner was getting pressure to sell and was going to lose a lot of tenants because this happened and more than likely be forced to sell. See who is pressuring to buy the trailer park and its valuable land on that highway corner, which has to be worth millions. Do that and I bet you find the slime on this one."

Sky nodded and smiled.

"See you for lunch," I said and jumped back to Sims and Canyon.

"What did she say?" Sims asked.

"Eating dinner with Detective Lawrence, couldn't say anything, but she nodded and smiled and I bet it will come up in the dinner conversation shortly."

"No bet," Sims said.

And we all drank to that and then explained to Canyon
why his comment more than likely would lead to the solution.

CHAPTER FORTY-ONE

S ims and I brought our own lunch to Sky's office, sandwiches that we had picked up on the way from a deli just off the Strip. Sky had opted for another cheeseburger and fries.

And she was smiling and eating when we arrived.

"How was dinner with Detective Lawrence?" I asked, dropping onto her couch.

"Productive," Sky said, a twinkle in her eye that made both Sims and I laugh.

"Productive meaning solving the case or more future dates?" I asked.

Sky just laughed. "Let's say both. He's a good guy. Kind of handsome in an old-guy sort of way."

"Both?" I asked. "So you got the people who took the bus?"

"Detective Lawrence arrested them about two hours ago," Sky said. "Two guys, both wanting to get the owner of the Sundowner to sell to their holding company. One hid on the bus, the other spent the day digging the hole with the backhoe at the construction site."

"I hope they toss the keys away," Sims said, disgusted.

"You know," Sky said, "it wouldn't hurt if you two pay them a visit a little later, give them a healthy dose of remorse to get them to confess."

I just applauded and Sims said, "Oh, that would be fun."

"How about we give them a little bit of their own medicine," I said. "We can implant in their minds that every time someone shuts off the lights, they feel like they are running out of air and suffocating."

Now it was Sky's turn to applaud and laugh.

Then she said, "Have I ever said how much I enjoy working with you two?"

"Anytime," I said.

"Are both the Youngs and the bus driver going to make it?" Sims asked.

"They are," Sky said. "Past the psychological issues, they will make a full recovery. And all three of them identified the two who did this to them."

"We might need to stop by the hospital a little later today and help them with those psychological problems," I said. "We can make them less painful at least."

Sims and Sky were both nodding.

"Crack in the skylight save them?" I asked.

"It did," Sky said. "It let just enough oxygen in to extend what they had. But they would not have made it another half day because they were out of water and food. Lucky you two stumbled across Brad Young."

"Lucky for them that I died a year ago today," I said. "And Sims died a few months later and we could be here to find Brad Young."

"If I had a drink," Sky said, "I'd drink to that."

"Planning on it later," Sims said, giving me that smile that I knew meant a lot more than a drink.

CHAPTER FORTY-TWO

After Sims and I did our errands at the jail and then the hospital, I decided what I wanted to do to celebrate the first anniversary of my death.

I wanted to get a good dinner, steak and lobster with a good wine, then go back to our wonderful condo and just make some great drinks and sit on our patio and enjoy the evening with Sims, the love of my life.

And maybe talk a little about the last year, but only in good ways.

Sims thought that was a perfect idea and so after a dinner that was sinfully good, we ended up back home on our patio looking out over downtown Las Vegas and the Strip beyond.

It was again a perfect night, not hot, not cold, just comfortable with no wind and even the tourists weren't making too much noise.

I don't think that in a year I had felt this relaxed and at home with myself and who I was. It took a year, but it seems I now knew who I was.

Canyon joined us after about thirty minutes, then Sky appeared.

And the laughter ramped up.

Thirty minutes later Jewel and Tommy appeared. Tommy had to pull a chair out from the kitchen.

"What do we call this?" Jewel asked, smiling at me. "And don't say death party."

"Celebration of life party," I said. "I can't begin to tell you all how lucky I feel to be sitting here, with the love of my life, with a life's mission to help people. I'll celebrate that every year."

They all raised their glasses in agreement.

And at that moment Poker Boy, Patty, and Lady Luck herself appeared just inside the open patio door and we had to move the party inside as I realized that Sims must have invited everyone.

Sims and I were the last to move inside and she was just standing there smiling at me.

I said softly, "Thank you."

"Just glad you died," she said, laughing softly.

"Yeah, me too," I said.

We stood there staring into each other's eyes.

Finally I said, "So now let's get on with another year of living."

"A grand idea," she said, hugging me.

And I hugged her back and then we turned to join our friends, ghosts and superheroes and gods alike, for a party to kick off the new year.

And wow, what a party it was.

DeanWesleySmithStore.Com

GET MORE
MARBLE GRANT

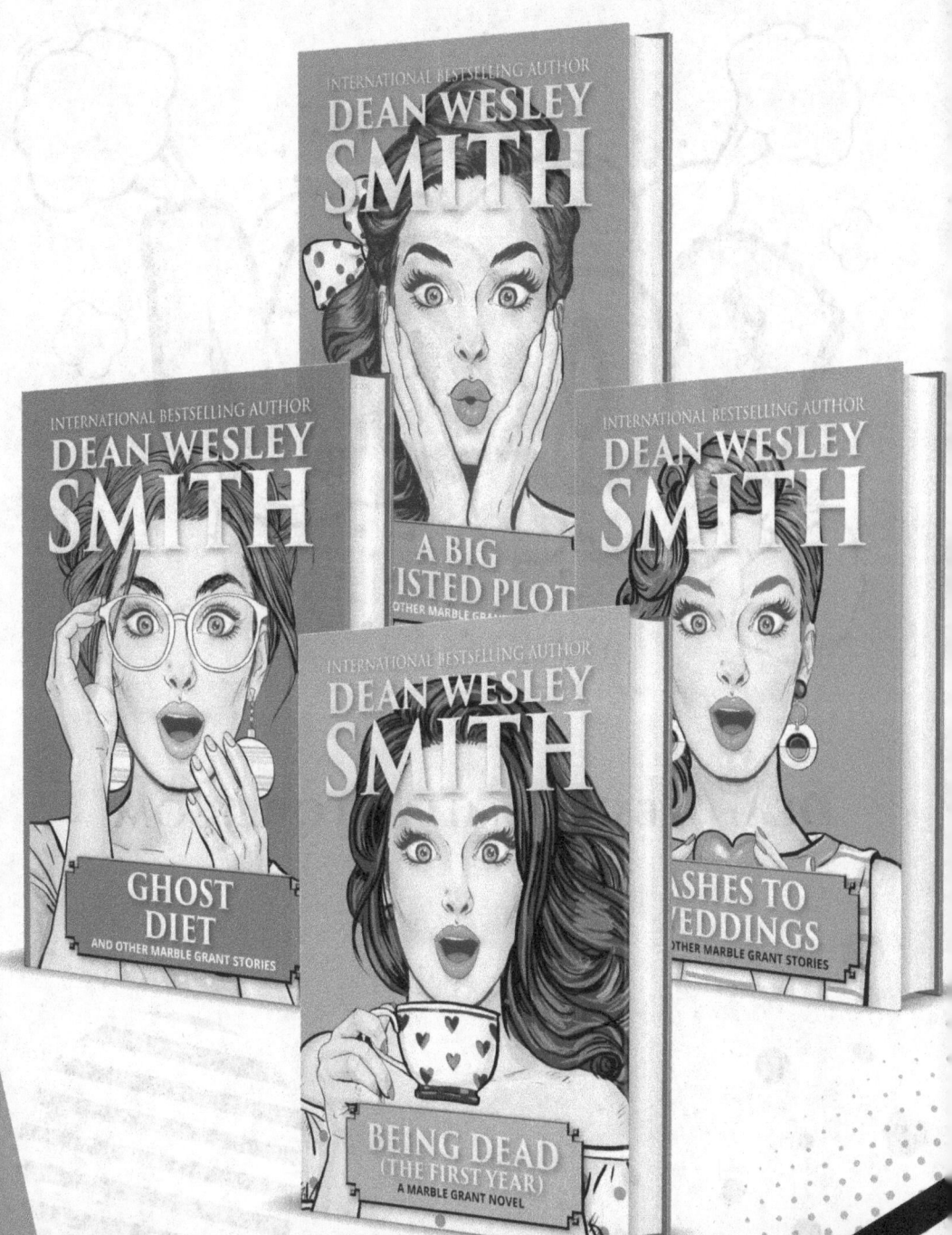

DEANWESLEYSMITHSTORE.COM

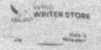

MARBLE GRANT
NO ONE HAS MORE FUN BEING DEAD

MARBLE GRANT
NO ONE HAS MORE FUN BEING DEAD

DeanWesleySmithStore.Com

DEAN WESLEY
SMITH

MARBLEGRANT.COM

MARBLE GRANT
NO ONE HAS MORE FUN BEING DEAD

HEAR FROM DEAN

Want More From Dean?

For Dean Wesley Smith's newsletter
go to deanwesleysmith.com.

Get the latest news and releases from all of WMG's authors
and lines, including Kristine Grayson, Kris Nelscott,
Pulphouse Magazine, and so much more...

To sign up, **go to wmgbooks.com.**

About the Author
Dean Wesley Smith

Considered one of the most prolific writers working in modern fiction, *New York Times* and *USA Today* bestselling writer, Dean Wesley Smith published over two hundred novels and over seven hundred books in forty years, and hundreds and hundreds of short stories. He has over thirty million copies of his books in print.

At the moment he produces novels in four major series, including the time travel **Thunder Mountain** novels set in the old west, the galaxy-spanning **Seeders Universe** series, the cold case mystery series, **Cold Poker Gang** series, and the superhero series staring **Poker Boy.**

During his career, Dean also wrote a couple dozen *Star Trek* novels, the only two original *Men in Black* novels, Spider-Man and X-Men novels, plus novels set in gaming and television worlds. Writing with his wife Kristine Kathryn Rusch under the name Kathryn Wesley, they wrote the novel for the NBC miniseries **The Tenth Kingdom** and other books for *Hallmark Hall of Fame* movies.

He wrote novels under dozens of pen names in the worlds

of comic books and movies, including novelizations of almost a dozen films, from *X-Men* to *The Final Fantasy* to *Steel* to *Rundown*.

Dean also worked as a fiction editor off and on, starting at Pulphouse Publishing, then at *VB Tech Journal*, then Pocket Books, and now at WMG Publishing where he and Kristine Kathryn Rusch serve as executive editors for the acclaimed *Fiction River* anthology series. He took over the editorship of the acclaimed *Pulphouse Magazine* in 2018.

For more information about Dean's books and ongoing projects, please visit his website at www.deanwesleysmith.com

f facebook.com/deanwsmith3

P patreon.com/deanwesleysmith

BB bookbub.com/authors/dean-wesley-smith

www.ingramcontent.com/pod-product-compliance
Lightning Source LLC
Chambersburg PA
CBHW010728100726
47899CB00009B/2977